MW01135900

The Challenger Deep

A Novel

Brian Melgar

Here's to the blank page.

The Challenger Deep Copyright © 2016 by Brian Maximiliano Melgar

All rights reserved. Printed in the United States of America. No part of this book may be used or reproduced in any manner whatsoever without written permission except in the case of brief quotations embodied in critical articles or reviews.

This book is a work of fiction. Names, characters, businesses, organizations, places, events and incidents either are the product of the author's imagination or are used fictitiously. Any resemblance to actual persons, living or dead, events, or locales is entirely coincidental.

For information contact: BrianMelgarPolanco@gmail.com

Book and Cover design by Scott "Fuzzy" Joseph
Edited by Devin McCrea

ISBN: 9781530713240

First Edition: May 2020

10 9 8 7 6 5 4 3 2 1

Contents

Dedications	7
Foreword	9
Prologue	12
Chapter 1	25
Chapter 2	47
Chapter 3	65
Chapter 4	84
Chapter 5	93
Chapter 6	110
Chapter 7	122
Chapter 8	136
Chapter 9	152
Chapter 10	174
Chapter 11	189
Chapter 12	210
Chapter 13	229
Acknowledgments	246

Dedications

To my mother and father, for their relentless support.

To Daniel, Savanna and Kristopher, for never abandoning me.

To Khristine, for loving all of my flaws.

I can only hope I've done you all proud.

Foreword

In 2016, I self-released a novel called *The Challenger Deep*. I was a 23-year-old fledgling writer. Sure, I had been writing recreationally for years at that point, but this was my first attempt to do something more than short stories that would never leave my digital drawer. The process of writing that first novel was nothing short of transcendent, like discovering an entirely new side of myself that I wasn't expecting to exist. It helped me move past personal issues that I had refused to acknowledge for years and contributed to my growth as a person, sending me one step forward into becoming the person that I had always wanted to be. I wanted to share this new me with the world, and I self-released the book on Amazon's platforms, a process I found very easy and accessible.

It took years of self-reflection and re-reading my own work to realize that I owed these characters more than I had given them the first time around. I owed them a better path, a better ending and a better explanation. One, in particular, deserved so much more than I was able (or willing) to give at the time. I resisted the idea that what I had written in 2016 wasn't complete and I resisted the idea that I had to update this novel to give everyone a chance to read it in its best possible incarnation. Thus, here we are, in 2020, and I'm finally listening to reason and passion.

Ladies and gentlemen, I give you the new and definitive *The Challenger Deep.*

BRIAN MELGAR

Prologue

As she walked around the room performing integrity checks on her camera equipment, she couldn't help but feel wonder at how far technology has come in her short lifespan. The inspection, for her, was more of a ritual than anything else. It was her moment to feel in awe that these jumbles of wires and metal could transmit from such depths, sending the terrestrial world images of the unknown planet that exists underseas. She lingered a little longer than usual, ensuring that all wires were connected properly, broadcasting a test transmission and double checking the router. It was time to give her superiors reason to celebrate. They were almost at their destination: the ocean floor — Earth's final and most deadly frontier.

Capturing a glance at herself in a nearby window, she adjusted her posture. While her standards of professional dress may vary day to day, it never hurt to appear consistent to her superiors. She was wearing a lab coat over her plain gray t-shirt and sweatpants, which she buttoned up with care. Pulling up her auburn hair and putting on a pair of glasses, she decided that the illusion was mostly complete. Once she was satisfied that everything looked in order, she put on her serious face and pressed RECORD.

"Year nine, month eleven, day three. This is Sasha Wilkins, reporting in. We've reached a depth of almost two leagues and expect to reach the bottom of the Challenger Deep by month's end. From there, we begin exploring the rest of the Mariana Trench and the surrounding ecosystem. Our vessel has continued to hold steady and there have been no complications since my last transmission. All in all, this journey has been more peaceful than we could have hoped. Should this continue, I feel we may be able to finish our preliminary exploration with full results sooner than expected. After which, we'll be able to send more scientists to other parts of the ocean floor. I will report back in three days, or sooner, should the need arise. Thank you."

Sasha hit the STOP button on the camera and shut it off before exhaling heavily. She detested performing these check-ins, but she tempered that dislike with the knowledge that her job wasn't all that challenging - yet. Her crew had the power of life and death in their hands, and she was just a scientist. But, what a time to be a scientist on the cutting edge! Ten years of work by some of the top engineers in the field of oceanic engineering had allowed this vessel to exist. A submarine that could not only handle unheard of amounts of oceanic pressure but could sustain human life simultaneously. A technological marvel. Twenty years ago, having both of those features - depth and the ability to sustain life - was impossible. At least, at the depths that Sasha and her team would be going to. It was made possible by the creation of a new type of synthetic metal, which was originally created by cell phone companies to make their devices nigh on indestructible.

As advanced as it was, the technology still had its compromises. With all submarines, the chief concern of the engineers creating the vessel is oceanic pressure. In this case, the concern was speed. Given enough descent time, the metal could evenly distribute the pressure of the ocean across the entire surface of the vessel - although they still hadn't figured out how to incorporate glass. A quick ascent or descent, however, would not provide enough time for pressure distribution, leading to what Sasha jokingly referred to as "recycling." In other words, the ship becomes a crushed soda can.

Once the "recycling" effect was explained to her, Sasha stopped asking questions about the submarine. The inner workings of their submarine wasn't what she was interested in; her attention was squarely placed on the creatures that dwelled in these depths. As long as her crew could keep her alive to see the ocean floor up close, she was content to live in ignorance of the particulars.

Being a part of this crew was the opportunity of a lifetime, but it had not come without its sacrifices. She and her husband hadn't been married long when this opportunity had presented itself. It wasn't easy to say goodbye, especially considering this mission was estimated to run for at least two decades. Her husband was a professor at their local community college and had been surprisingly understanding and accepting of her desire to take the voyage. Both of their lives had been less than extraordinary, and this was something that neither of them had dreamed could happen. He encouraged her to follow this dream, and she knew how much it killed him to do so. They had not been allowed to communicate for the duration of their trip downwards, but she had been assured that once they conclude their exploration and begin their ascent, communications could be established between the two. She needed to be completely focused on the mission in the meantime.

With her check-in concluded, Sasha decided to make a stop at the engine room to see Bobbi, a member of their crew with whom she had become close. It was important to make friends on long voyages like this.

After almost ten years, Sasha knew the layout of this submarine as if it were her own house. To reach the engine room, she would have to walk fifteen feet down the hall, turn left into the stairwell, down two flights, turn left onto the second to last floor of the submarine, turn right when you get to the hall, twenty feet forward, and turn left into the engine room. She could almost do it with her eyes closed, which was amazing given the size of this thing. It was 120 feet long and had 5 floors total. The width was about 40 feet, give or take a few inches. The first few months, she found herself getting lost all the time and having to radio Bobbi to help her find her way. Bobbi had been on the team that constructed the submarine, so knew the layout pretty damn well.

She opened the door to the engine room and saw that Bobbi was there, looking over a piece of paper with Albert, their lead engineer.

"Hey guys," Sasha said, not stopping to ask for admittance.

They both turned to face her. For some reason, Albert had a worried expression on his face. He had a piece of paper in his hand, most likely a printout, that he held behind his back. Of Spanish descent, Albert was an older man, in his late 50s, with fair skin and dark hair and a graying goatee that he clearly put a lot of effort into maintaining. Considerably less effort was put into hiding the fact that he was balding, but he pulled it off with the grace of a professional man. He was in good shape, due to the physical nature of running around a submarine, constantly putting out metaphorical fires.

"Mrs. Wilkins," he said, in a thick accent that was sometimes difficult to understand. He sounded overly professional. That was odd for him.

"Hey Sash," said Bobbi, a short and stocky African American woman. Somewhere in her mid to late 40s, she was one of the kindest people Sasha had ever met. She kept her head shaved, and when Sasha asked her why, she said that hair was difficult to maintain on a voyage like this, which had made Sasha consider shaving her own head. Bobbi also, for some reason, had a concerned look on her face.

"What's going on?" Sasha asked.

Bobbi and Albert exchanged a look that worried Sasha. They looked genuinely frightened by whatever they had been discussing before Sasha's unceremonious entrance.

"Nothing you need to worry about just yet. Just make sure you're ready for what's coming. Hopefully, this will all be worth it," Albert replied. That was ominous.

"We actually have some work to do right now, Sash. We'll let you know if we need you to take a look at anything, though," Bobbi said, "In the meantime, why don't you go get some sleep? You look tired."

"Alright, if you're sure..." replied Sasha.

"I am. Sleep tight, Sash," Bobbi said. They both quickly turned around and continued looking over the slip of paper.

Although the look on their faces was concerning, Sasha decided to trust Bobbi. If it was something serious, Bobbi would tell her. Perhaps not publicly, but that was ok. This seemed pretty confidential, and whatever it is, it has them spooked. Bobbi would hopefully spill the beans eventually. All Sasha could do was wait.

She slowly made her way up to the barracks and laid in her bunk. She slept, and her dreams were as blank and dark as the depths that she would soon find herself in.

One Month Later

"After ten years, we've reached the depths of the ocean floor. The Challenger Deep. We can finally begin."

Sasha had just sent the transmission letting her superiors know that they had reached their destination. It was finally time. She is a part of the first crew to ever make it to such an extreme depth and she couldn't contain her excitement. Now comes the best part: the exploration. It was time to start making discoveries with the potential to change the world.

Before Sasha could begin her assignment, the submarine had to be calibrated to travel horizontally along the ocean floor. Sasha didn't know the specifics of it, but from what she understood, they were using an auxiliary engine to keep them 30 feet from the floor at all times, meaning that no matter what depth they travel along, they will remain a consistent distance from the surface. From there, they should be able to examine any creatures they find with minimal interruption to the natural ecosystem.

Sasha was making her way to the observatory on the bottom floor of the sub. Using sonar was currently their only option for visibility, but it was highly advanced sonar, allowing the team to detect any movement and determine the size of any creature they found. They could then use that same sonar to construct a digital image of the creature that would be alarmingly accurate. If what the sonar image showed seemed like something that should be studied further, they have a mechanism coated in the strengthened mineral that could grab it and bring it on board. Of course, they'd have to collect samples of the ocean water nearby first so they could build a tank to accurately mimic the local ecosystem for the specimens to survive in. Lastly, they would map out the ocean floor.

"Hey Bobbi," Sasha said into her transmitter, "Get in here, we're ready to get this party started."

"Alright, I'm on my way," came Bobbi's reply.

Sasha walked over to the controls for the sonar and the pulse waves, anxious. She had fantasized about this moment every day for the last ten years. She had fantasized about what they might find down here, what kind of strange and amazing animals might live this far down, and what studying them could do for the people on land. These creatures could hold the genetic keys for curing cancer, diabetes... and it would all be thanks to this crew.

Bobbi walked into the observatory a few moments later. Sasha hadn't inquired about the secretive way that Bobbi and Albert had been behaving the previous month. She had decided it would be better to trust Bobbi and not pry. Truthfully, at this particular moment, that didn't matter at all. Bobbi was in charge of the pulse wave, setting it off at the proper intervals and with the proper magnitude, and Sasha's job was to observe the sonar readings, creating a layout of where they are and spotting any irregularities or life forms.

"All right, let's finally get this show on the road," said Bobbi.

And with that, Bobbi set off the first pulse wave. Sasha didn't expect the way it shook the submarine itself, the sensation of a deep vibration under her feet. Regardless of the shock, she kept her eyes trained on the sonar. It mapped out the ground beneath them for the next mile or so, and the depth of the floor was consistent, give or take a few feet in some areas. With no signs of any life forms just yet, the submarine kept moving forward.

Thirty seconds later, Bobbi set off the second pulse wave and again, the one-mile radius around them was mapped out. To the left of them was a steady ascent in depth, about 50 feet or so. They were slowly exiting the Challenger Deep and making their way further into the Mariana Trench, but there were still no signs of life. They kept moving along the deeper surface, intentionally avoiding where the floor started to rise.

After one full minute, Bobbi set off the third pulse. This one shook the submarine a little more than the last two, and surprised Sasha enough to look away from the sonar.

"What was that?" Sasha asked.

"I slipped. Pay attention to the sonar," Bobbi said in a stern voice.

Sasha turned her attention back to the sonar to see something in the corner of the image. A slight rise, but it didn't look like part of the floor. It was about a mile in front of them.

"I think I see something," Sasha said calmly, "Right there, almost out of our range."

Sasha heard Bobbi whisper something into her transmitter before the submarine started moving forward at a slightly faster pace than before. About 15 seconds later, Bobbi set off another pulse wave, about as strong as the last one had been. This time, Sasha didn't take her eyes off of the sonar image.

"No way... is that..." Sasha whispered.

"What do you see, Sash?" Bobbi asked.

"It... it looks like a hand," Sasha replied.

Sasha kept intently watching the image, all the while being filled with a sense of dread. Whatever this was, it looked raised, too close to them.

She had barely finished that thought when the Submarine jolted violently to one side. Sasha was knocked to the ground and hit her head against one of the tables on her way down. Her vision became blurry as she fought to try to stand back up. Red lights began flashing all around and she could hear the emergency siren. Sasha grabbed the side of the table she had hit and pulled herself up to see that Bobbi hadn't fallen and was still manning the pulse wave, now setting it off again.

"Bobbi! What are you doing?!" Sasha screamed.

Bobbi turned around and gave Sasha a serious look, "My job," she said.

Sasha stumbled to her feet, terrified. She started running for the door when Albert walked through it, more calmly than she would have expected. He grabbed her roughly by the arms and dragged her back to the sonar station. He forced her to take control of it again and look at it. With Bobbi constantly setting off pulse waves, the image of the hand was clearer than ever. And she could see that it was now directly below them.

"I want you to see this, Mrs. Wilkins. The real reason we came down here," Albert said, as Sasha saw that the hand was closer than in the previous image. It looked like it was going to grab them!

"We are not the dominant species on this planet, Mrs. Wilkins. We were not meant to inherit the earth. We were not made in God's image. They were."

She felt the submarine stop jolting, the hand now closed around it, tightening.

"And now... they are awake," Albert said, as the hand crushed the submarine.

Chapter 1

Jeremiah slowly awoke to the sound of his obnoxious alarm.

Groggily, he reached for the cell phone sitting on the nightstand to shut it off. At this hour, it sounded like harpies screeching in his ear, making him more irritable than he should be. He'd been meaning to change the sound for weeks, but he was constantly putting it off, always regretting it the following morning, without fail.

He slowly sat up on his bed, his bones creaking in a near harmony with the sound of his groans from being awoken at such an unreasonable hour. He looked at the cell phone in his hand. 5:00AM. Why he chose to wake up at this hour when he wasn't expected at work until 9:00AM was a decision that still baffled him. Reluctantly, he stood up and moved towards his closet, directly to the right of his king-sized bed. He grabbed a pair of running shorts from his drawer that sat beneath where his regular clothes hung. He then sifted through his clothes until he found his black pullover sweater. He quickly pulled both on and went back to sit on his bed. The socks he wore the day before were on the floor, next to his running shoes. He may as well use those again as he had only worn them around the house after taking a shower and they weren't dirty just yet. Probably. He put on his socks, laced his shoes, grabbed his cell phone and some earphones and was out the door.

He had been running for years. Pretty much ever since Sasha left. Before then, they had always been pretty active together. They went on hikes, played sports and went on bike rides together. He had harbored a fear that his wife would come home to an excessively pudgy husband, so he had taken up this running routine every morning to keep that from happening. It was an extremely annoying habit, but it was worth it. At 42, he was staving off most symptoms of being middle aged, his graying hair notwithstanding. Truthfully, that's why he chose to keep it clean shaven.

One mile a day around the suburbs was the normal circuit that he ran, but today he chose to go for two miles. It's not like it would make him late to work, anyway; he woke up entirely too early for that to be a problem. He waved to his elderly neighbor Mrs. Anna as she collected the newspaper from her driveway. She somberly waved back before proceeding inside her house. Mrs. Anna had lost her dog a few days ago. She had had one child many years ago who never visited her, had never married and had always lived alone with her dog who had lived to be about 15 years old. Jeremiah suspected that her dog was one of the last things that she had that made her cling to life. He made a mental note to visit her later this week, it could do her some good to have company. After fifteen minutes, his phone vibrated to let him know that he had finished his two miles, and he began to make his way back home.

He entered through his front door and locked it behind him, pausing to look into his house. It seemed too big today. His living room was dark, and he could barely see his enormous couch situated in front of the wall mounted 52" TV over the fireplace. There wasn't much else to observe, just a small entertainment center that housed various Blu-Rays and DVDs. Next to that was a kitchen that he had forced himself to learn how to use properly to cook his own meals. Another annoying habit that ended up paying off for him, health-wise.

He made his way up the stairs and made a right turn into the master bathroom so he could take a shower and get ready for the day's labors. He turned the light on, undressed, set the water to hot, and stepped inside. He quickly cleaned himself without much thought before turning the water off and grabbing the "His" towel from the "His & Hers" set he had by the sink. A cheesy idea, definitely, but Sasha had insisted on them. She was a strange person, caught somewhere between making fun of couples like those and secretly wanting to be a part of one of those couples. He toweled himself off, wrapped the towel around his waist and made his way across the hall into his bedroom.

He switched the light on and walked towards his closet to pick his clothes for the day. His profession mandated that he look presentable at all times, but the line between professional and casual was one he liked to jump rope with on a daily basis. He opted for a pair of jeans, dress shoes, an un-tucked button up shirt and a black blazer. Just casual enough for him to get his kicks, just professional enough that no one would give him any grief for it.

Dressed and ready, Jeremiah checked his cell phone. It was still only 7:00AM. He had about an hour and a half before he had to begin making his way to work, so he figured he'd take the rest of his morning ritual slowly, just as he liked it. First and most importantly, he needed to make himself some breakfast. He walked downstairs and turned right into his living room, picking up the remote and turning his TV on before continuing to walk into the kitchen. Turning the light on, he opened his fridge to determine what he should make for himself. He settled on a thick piece of ham, two eggs and some orange juice.

He cooked quietly as he listened to the sounds from the TV. It was some news report about an Astronaut who had just returned from a mission to Mars. Good for him, making it back home. Jeremiah chose to eat his meal in the kitchen as well. There was something calming about eating standing up, rather than sitting down. It was one of those odd preferences that Sasha had always made fun of him for, but he'd always enjoyed it. He didn't really know why.

After eating, he washed his dishes and the pan he used to cook the ham and eggs, knowing he wouldn't want to have a mess to clean up when he got home from work. He turned off the kitchen light and walked into the living room, which was only illuminated by the TV. The ambient noise and lighting were just relaxing enough that he could wind down from the morning run, but not so relaxing that he would fall back asleep. He changed the input of the TV from CABLE to INTERNET and used the web browser to get to the website of his favorite podcast. It was a daily half hour long nerd culture discussion by two comic book writers. He had never read any of their books himself, but he liked their insight, and their discussions were always entertaining to listen to. It was almost like watching the news, but instead of being a depressing reminder of reality, it was a quirky and entertaining way to start the day and elevate one's mood.

The podcast ended, and Jeremiah checked his phone again for the time. 8:15AM. A little early, but if he didn't leave now, he'd make himself restless pacing back and forth. He shut off the TV, grabbed his keys from the countertop in the kitchen, and left through his front door.

He unlocked his car, stepped inside and started it. He'd had this Toyota Prius for about five years now and he really liked it. If Sasha had been here when he decided to buy a Prius, she would have never let him hear the end of it. Little victories. But it was a reliable car that got him where he needed to go, and he didn't have to spend as much as other people on gas. Besides, anything is better than the piece of crap Dodge Intrepid he and Sasha had foolishly purchased before they got married. That thing had left them stranded more often than it had gotten them to their destination. Jeremiah had lost count of how much money they had spent fixing it only for it to break down on them again a week after the fact.

He normally liked to drive with some music on, but he didn't feel the desire to put any on today. He decided to drive in silence to work. It was about a twenty-minute drive, depending on traffic, to the local community college where he worked as a professor.

The beginning of today's agenda was to teach a Creative Writing class. The English department head had decided that a Creative Writing class would be good for their student body, nurturing their imaginative side and all that, and had asked him to teach it. Jeremiah accepted, but only because he had no intention of feeding these kids any bullshit about what writing is like. Jeremiah had tried his hand at professional writing once upon a time and had published one book. It was received well, and he has since been asked to write a sequel, but he felt that he should keep writing as his private hobby, rather than attempting to monetize it. Once you start making money from your hobby, it adds all kinds of pressure to something that's supposed to be relieving and cathartic.

As a tenured professor, he would be able to teach this creative writing class the way he felt it should be taught. He'll tell these kids what he wished someone had told him when he was first starting out as an amateur writer. Of course, they wouldn't see it that way, more than likely viewing him as a disillusioned one-hit wonder, but he would be doing them a favor in the long run.

Jeremiah parked in his official spot, not far from the classroom he was meant to be teaching in, turned off his car, grabbed his teaching materials that he always kept in his car and started walking. Ever since he got tenure, he'd gotten more relaxed in his teaching style, opting to improvise more often than not. It seemed to work for him, and he hasn't received any complaints from his students thus far.

He made it to his classroom with fifteen minutes to spare. He decided to take the time to think about what he was going to say and settled on writing a single word on the white board behind him, that word being:

"Write." That's all he needed for now, so he sat at his desk and waited.

A few students started trickling in about ten minutes before class was set to start. Jeremiah decided to keep quiet until it was officially time to begin his lecture. Teaching was a performance to him, more like being a musician onstage than anything else. It gave him a rush of adrenaline, and he especially needed to feel that rush today. He almost couldn't stop checking the time on his phone. It took way too long for the time to finally become 9:00AM. But when the clock finally complied with his lack of patience, he was more than ready to begin.

Jeremiah stood up and looked over the classroom. There were somewhere between 35 to 40 students here. 35 to 40 students who had enrolled in this class thinking they were about to be given the keys to the kingdom of creating worthwhile literature. Unfortunately, it was time they learn that those keys, like the work they'd be doing, were nothing but fiction. He cleared his throat before beginning.

"My name is Professor Wilkins. Welcome to Creative Writing. Most of you probably enrolled in this class because you want to learn how to write. At least, I'm assuming so, considering this is an elective. If you're here for any other reason, I recommend not wasting your time. For the rest of you, I'm going to let you in on a dirty little secret. I cannot teach you how to write."

Jeremiah paused to survey the class and gauge their reactions.

"Writing isn't something that can be taught. It's something that is practiced, and practiced, and practiced until maybe, eventually, hopefully... you write something worth reading. That's something that people need to understand. People claim to be writers, write one awful piece of literature, if you can call it that, receive some criticism... and quit. Just like that.

See, today's writers, and I use the term 'writer' very loosely, don't have thick enough skin to withstand the process of becoming a real writer. You're going to write shit, you're going to get crushed, and you're going to have to keep going."

Some of the students were starting to look a bit taken aback by this lecture. Maybe by the content, or maybe by the language he was using. Either way, they were being affected and that was good.

"To be a writer, you have to pay your dues. You have to write the bad stuff and get the criticism. And you have to learn from every bad thing you've ever written. You can't look at the bad reviews and let it get you down. You have to read those reviews, those criticisms, and learn from them. What did you do well? What did you do wrong? How can you improve on your next work? You have to ask yourself these questions if you ever hope to make it as a writer, whatever that means."

Jeremiah had hit his stride. His hope was that he would discourage the disingenuous and encourage the ones with true passion.

"So, for those of you that came here, hoping I would teach you how to write, I'm sorry, but I cannot do that for you. All I can do is read your writing and give you some real and honest feedback. If it sucks, I will tell you. If it's mediocre, I will tell you. And if, by some miracle, it's good, I will tell you. The one and only lesson I can impart is simply one word," Jeremiah continued, then pointed to the single word he had written on the white board, "Write! Now, write me some shit, you have the next hour to come up with something to show me. No syllabus discussion, no grade break-down. Just write. I'll be at my desk, waiting to be impressed."

And with that, Jeremiah sat back at his desk, reached into the bag that housed his teaching materials, took out a notebook and a pen, and settled in to write something himself. He can't rightfully give his students advice on how to be a writer and not take the advice himself.

"Excuse me, Professor Wilkins?" said a male student sitting in the front row.

Jeremiah looked up from his notebook to see the student, a young man in his early twenties. He was a bit on the heavier side and was dressed in a black graphic t-shirt and jeans. "Yes?" asked Jeremiah.

"You have a lot to say about being a writer, but I did my research on you. You've only ever had one book published. Yeah, people liked it, but it was just one. I think that you're just a one-hit wonder trying to capitalize on some kids wanting to be more. And your lesson plan? Are we just going to be coming here to sit quietly for an hour and a half twice a week? Not only are you capitalizing on us, but you're also wasting our time on your laziness and unwillingness to teach us," said the student.

Jeremiah was a bit surprised. Not at what he said, but that he truly believed that Jeremiah was being lazy.

"You can use whatever excuse you want to make yourself feel like you don't have to go through the trouble of becoming a legitimate writer, son. But what I've told you today is the absolute truth. No one can teach you how to write. Anyone who says differently is just blowing smoke up your ass and collecting your money," Jeremiah stood up then,

"I'm simply telling you the truth, nothing sugar coated about it. You want to be a writer? Then write. Writing isn't my profession, young man. Teaching is. Writing is a hobby of mine. I haven't had anything published since my first novel by choice."

Jeremiah felt his emotions get the better of him. On this day, of all days, one of his new students decides to set him off. This was not the day to test him.

"So, if all you're looking for is to humiliate a man who is being straight with you out of respect, then, bravo. You've done that. But, and this is against my better judgment, if you want to become a better writer, then sit your ass down and WRITE!"

Jeremiah looked out at all of their stunned faces. The chubby male student was surprised at the rant Jeremiah had just gone on. He had nothing to say now, it seemed. Jeremiah went to his desk, put away his belongings, and started heading for the door.

"Get my email from the college website. Email me whatever you write. Or don't. See you in two days," and with that, he left the classroom.

Jeremiah didn't look back. He headed for his office on the opposite side of campus, figuring he'd send the students on his list an email with the syllabus and the grading scale, as a courtesy. That way they'd have his email, and they knew what was expected of them in this class. He made it to his office, shut the door behind him, and sat at his desk. His office was depressingly small. Just enough room to have his desk, two chairs, and a small bookshelf behind him. He had occupied that bookshelf with random ones that he had purchased at a yard sale. Truth be told, he hadn't read most of them, he just wanted to fill up space, as he felt it made his office look more professional this way. He would have filled it with books he'd read, but he had a tendency to re-read books and didn't want to have to make a trip to his office every time the urge struck.

Jeremiah pulled his laptop out from his teaching bag and set it in front of him. He loaded up the school's website, logged in with his faculty account and accessed the files for his current students, deciding to send a mass email to all of them. He attached the semester's syllabus along with the grading scale for the course. The grading would basically be done on whether or not the students wrote anything. He wouldn't grade based on quality, just on if they wrote something. His primary goal was to get people to write, and this was the best way to do it.

Not long after he hit SEND on the mass email, there was a knock at his office door.

"Come in," Jeremiah said. Dreading what it could possibly be. His tolerance for interaction had just been depleted by the encounter in his class. The door opened and in walked his boss, the Dean of the school, Edgar Brown. This should be good.

"Jeremiah, do you have a minute? There's something I'd like to discuss with you."

Of course he did, "Sure Edgar, take a seat. What's going on?"

"A student just came by my office. He said there was some sort of altercation in your class today. Which you should still be in, by the way," Dean Brown said.

"I'm actually pretty amazed that he already had the time to meet with you and tell you about it, considering he's a bit on the heavy side."

"This is not the time for jokes, Jerry," Dean Brown said sternly. He knew Jeremiah hated being called Jerry.

"Look... Professor Wilkins... I know today is a rough day for you. But you can't let your emotions take over you like that. You're supposed to be a professional educator. You let a snot nosed punk set you off today. I understand how hard it is," Dean Brown said.

"No. You really don't, Eddie," this time Jeremiah used one of Dean Brown's hated nicknames.

"You don't know what it's like to wait ten years just to hear that your wife died. You don't know what it's like, hoping for the day you can speak to her again, and when that call finally comes, it turns out to be an unfamiliar voice telling you that your wife, your best friend, has died due to 'complications.' You don't know what it's like to wonder how long she'd even been dead before anyone bothered to fucking tell you! Don't you *dare* pretend you understand. A year ago, on this day, some government official who didn't know me or my wife told me in a deadpan voice that my wife was *dead*. Until that's happened to you, you don't understand how hard it is."

This marked the second time Jeremiah had left someone in shock today. Coming to work was a bad idea. Just because he had tenure didn't mean he could get away with talking to his boss like that.

"You know what? Go home, Jeremiah. You won't be disciplined. Just... just take the day off. You shouldn't be at work on a day like this. I'll smooth things over with the student. He'll probably drop your class. Just relax today, alright? Come back in when your class meets next," said Dean Brown, and then he promptly left the office.

Jeremiah sat back in his chair and expelled a sigh. That went surprisingly well, all things considered. People don't generally get away with screaming at their bosses. He was right, though. He needed to go home and relax. This was a day for mourning, and he should have been smart enough to recognize that. Something within him, probably pride, had held him back from realizing that a day like this is not one to take lightly. He looked at the clock on his desk and saw that it was only 9:30AM. He packed up his laptop, stood up, walked out through his office door, shutting and locking it behind him.

***

It was another quiet drive. Again, Jeremiah opted to not listen to any music. He didn't really think of anything as he drove. He should be mourning his wife, but he couldn't bring himself to start thinking about that right now. He knew he'd just break down while driving. So, he emptied his mind, promising himself that he would deal with it when he got home.

After twenty minutes, he reached his house. He parked in his driveway, exited his car, leaving the teaching materials in the passenger seat once again, and made his way inside. As soon as he locked the door behind him, he felt himself break down. He fell to his knees right in front of his front door and began weeping. Ten years of waiting, ten years of being so proud of his wife, only to learn that she had died. The worst part was that he had no idea what she had looked like at the time of her death. They had both aged, but they hadn't done it together the way that they had planned it.

Jeremiah positioned himself to sit against the wall perpendicular to his front door, weeping silently, remembering what he could about his late wife. He thought of her auburn hair, tied into a ponytail on a lazy Sunday afternoon. He thought of how she would always start reading a book without her glasses on, which made her squint her eyes at the text before she decided to grab her glasses and put them on. All of her little habits and quirks that made her the woman he loved. And she had died, without him, 36,000 feet under the ocean.

Jeremiah opened his eyes in time to see something fall next to him. A letter. Someone had slipped it through the mail slot in his door. This wasn't the regular time that he received his mail. He picked it up and examined the simple white envelope, with nothing written or printed on it. There was no return address and even Jeremiah's own address wasn't on it. He turned it around to find it was being held closed by a blank red seal. There was nothing to identify where this envelope had come from.

Looking at this envelope gave Jeremiah a strange feeling in the pit of his stomach. He slowly broke the seal and opened it. Inside was a simple white piece of paper. He unfolded it slowly and held it up to read what it said:

"J,

Leave your porch light on tonight if you want to know what happened.

-A Friend."

***

She didn't like leaving her house more than she had
to. Unfortunately, cereal doesn't really have the same
charm when it isn't accompanied by milk, so here she
was, perusing the seemingly infinite options available
for those in search of dairy. She wondered, very briefly,
what the difference between all of the different brands
of milk were. The thought didn't last long, as she
quickly went for store brand 2% milk. Jana was a lot of
things, and pragmatist was absolutely chief among
them.

She set the milk down in her cart, letting the door
that kept the cold temperatures in the store freezer
where it was meant to be close. As she did, she caught a
glimpse of something in the glass's reflective surface. It
looked like a face, but... it was wrong somehow.

She gasped and turned around as quickly as she
could, but there was no one anywhere near her. The
shoppers all seemed blissfully unaware of Jana's
existence as they filled their carts, and she took note of
how alone she truly was. So then, what was that face?

Another quality that Jana possessed in huge amounts
- paranoia. As quickly as her panicked legs would allow,
Jana finished shopping for other odds and ends she had
hastily scribbled down on her notepad and made her
way to the register. There had been no one behind her,

and there still seemed to be no one following, but that didn't change the fact that Jana had seen *something*, and she now felt *someone* following her.

When she finally reached the cash register, she practically threw her money at the poor and unsuspecting employee. He couldn't have been any older than 17, and here he was having to deal with Jana's paranoid episode.

As soon as that interaction ended, Jana could have sworn she flew out of the store and into her car, almost forgetting her groceries in the process. Even so, it wasn't fast enough.

Here's the thing about rearview mirrors: they are horribly frightening things. Sometimes, people don't want to know what's behind them, and other times, knowing that there's nothing there can make the feeling of being watched even worse.

Luckily, it wasn't long until Jana found herself parked in her driveway, and the sprint to her front door began. All whilst carrying the cursed groceries that had led her away from the safety of her home and into the uncertainty of the outside world.

As soon as she was inside of her home, Jana slammed her door shut and locked it comprehensively. One look at the door that kept the horrors of the world at bay told all the story one needed to know about the woman who resided within. More locks than anyone could bother to count kept any would-be intruders away. But it also kept the recluse inside, more often than not.

Jana didn't like leaving her house more than she had to. And this latest excursion had proven exactly why. For so long, Jana had felt that there was something lurking around the corner, lying in wait for her to drop her guard. And, as a result, she hadn't dropped her guard in many years.

But this was different. She saw something. She knows that she did. But she had no idea what it was or what it wanted.

But that *face.* She now had a face to go with the feeling. And it terrified her even more.

Chapter 2

Jeremiah read the letter in his hand a few more times, unsure of what it meant. If this were some kind of mystery movie, he would assume that it had something to do with his wife. That couldn't be what this is, could it? He opened his front door and looked around for signs of someone skulking around. He listened intently, but all he could hear was his neighbor's Pomeranian dog shrieking in that high-pitched bark that it always did. He might've been able to hear something, but that dog made sure he couldn't.

Filled with a sense of futility, Jeremiah closed and locked his door, a strange feeling overcoming him. If this was a prank being pulled on him, it was in terribly poor taste, considering the date. But if this was something serious, he had to know. He had always had his doubts about the circumstances surrounding the death of his wife. The government employee who had called to tell him that his wife was dead had given him no information other than that there were complications with the vessel once it reached the Challenger Deep.

He gave the letter another once-over. There was nothing abnormal about it, no defining characteristics, nothing to make him think this was something special. But still, there was no way he could ignore this. With a moment's hesitation, he lifted his hand up to the light switch and with a slight tremble, he turned on the porch light. And with that, he moved to the living room without turning on the light, sat on his couch, and began to wait.

***

Jeremiah sat in his living room, the only light coming from his TV. He had gotten a bit antsy sitting in silence for so long and decided that he needed some white noise to keep from going insane. At about 5:30PM, it had started to rain outside. It was strange, the weather had been acting up quite a bit lately. It was now 7:00PM, and still there was no one knocking on his door. He was starting to think that a cruel joke had been played on him. *Calm down, Jeremiah,* he thought to himself. *The note said TONIGHT, not today, there's still a chance the letter is real.* Despite the self-affirmations, it was hard to remain optimistic, especially considering how strange these circumstances were. He felt like he was slowly turning into the main character in some cheesy TV pilot that he'd laugh off and never watch again.

The news was on, but Jeremiah wasn't really paying attention. His mind was preoccupied, running through every tired fictional cliché that he could possibly have stumbled into. Maybe there was an underground group of freedom fighters trying to take down political tyranny and expose government secrets. Jeremiah chuckled. He was pretty sure he'd read that one before. Hell, he'd probably written that one before.

Before long, the clock struck 8:00PM and Jeremiah began to lose hope that anyone would arrive and give him some sort of explanation. Just as the thought crossed his mind, he heard his doorbell ring and his heart leapt into his throat at the sound. Jeremiah quickly rose from his couch and made his way to his front door. He looked through the peephole and saw a man wearing a raincoat, his face obscured by the hood. He couldn't really make out any significant features, but he looked suspicious. Jeremiah should've been cautious, but his heart was beating out of his chest and he couldn't contain himself.

He opened his front door and looked the man in the raincoat up and down. He was average height, something like 5 foot 8. It was hard to tell from below the rain coat, but he looked to be pretty skinny, not exactly built to be an underground soldier. So much for that little idea he had had earlier. The man in front of him walked into his house, closed the door behind him and removed the hood from over his head, revealing a Caucasian man who looked to be in about his mid-40s, with balding brown hair and some significantly pronounced worry lines on his forehead. Jeremiah recognized him.

"You're Peter Jacobson," Jeremiah said.

Peter Jacobson was a rather infamously known government whistleblower. He was responsible for leaking various documents and unsigned bills onto the internet, causing uproar among the people. He had been imprisoned for his activities no less than five times. He'd been reported missing about six months ago and was wanted for theft and conspiracy. It looks like 'missing' is not an applicable term in this case.

"That I am," Peter replied, "And you're Jeremiah Wilkins. Husband of the late Sasha Wilkins, who died onboard the unnamed vessel near the Challenger Deep."

Jeremiah was about to ask how Peter knew that, but then he remembered who the person in front of him was. Of course he knew about it. He had connections in all the right places, and rumor had it that he paid them all exceptionally well for the information they provided.

"That's right," Jeremiah replied, "You're the one who left the letter?"

"No, it wasn't me. I sent someone else to drop it off for me. I'm sure you're aware that people you don't want to come after you are looking for me. And I'd rather not go to such a public and suburban area more than once. This seems like the kind of neighborhood that has some seriously nosey people living here, and seeing a strange man in a raincoat showing up here more than once is probably enough for them to start talking, am I right?"

Jeremiah nodded his head. That was about the way things worked in this area.

"That's what I thought. So, I paid someone else to drop it off for me. Bought him a mailman costume to do so. Nothing suspicious about a mailman dropping off mail," Peter said.

"Unless it's at ten in the morning. Mail is delivered here at around four in the afternoon."

"Well, there's that little slip up. Nobody's perfect."

"The letter says that you know what happened. Since you mentioned my late wife, I'm assuming that you're talking about what happened to her," Jeremiah said.

"Yeah, that was slightly exaggerated."

"So, you don't know what happened?" Jeremiah pressed.

"I just said I was exaggerating. But, I'm on the trail of something. Something big, and the vessel your wife was on is at the center of it. I'm sure of it," Peter responded.

"What are you *talking* about?"

"Isn't it strange that such a publicized voyage stopped being reported on once it was launched? That its destruction received no media coverage, and it seemed to just get swept under the rug? When that vessel was destroyed, the government knew *immediately*. But they didn't even let any of the next of kin know until three months later. *Three months.* Your wife had been dead for three months before anyone even bothered to let you know. In such a connected society where every major event is immediately trending on Twitter, doesn't it seem weird that this didn't get so much as a column inch in an article?"

Jeremiah was stunned. His wife had been dead for three months before he got the call. He suspected that they had waited to tell him, but he had no idea that it was that long. He couldn't even focus on the rest of what Peter had said. He felt sick to his stomach.

"So... Why are you telling me? Have you told any of the other people who lost loved ones on that vessel?" Jeremiah asked.

"Oh, definitely not. I've been keeping an eye on everyone who lost someone. They all became depressed, lazy and fat. Some of them even killed themselves afterwards. You're the only one who didn't lose his marbles after learning what happened. You kept yourself on the up and up. You may have noticed, I'm not exactly the image of physical health. I'm... I'm sick. And I need someone to help me expose whatever it is that they're trying to hide."

"Wait, you're sick?" Jeremiah asked.

"I need your help. I have an isolated house a few miles from here that I paid someone to rent out for me. Come with me, I'll show you what I have so far, and I'll explain what we have to do. I can't do this by myself," Peter said.

Jeremiah hesitated for a moment. This seemed like the kind of thing most people would have to be out of their minds to agree to. But Peter Jacobson has never been wrong about the things he's exposed before. And he needed to know what really happened to his wife. He owed himself and his wife that closure. He knew what he had to say.

"Okay."

***

"Why is Mr. Wilkins' porch light still on? He never has it on this late."

"I don't know why you even know his porch light routine, Judy. Just leave it alone," Replied her husband.

Judy ignored her husband Paul. He never worried about anything. Judy was just about to call Mr. Wilkins and let him know that he had left his porch light on, when she saw his front door open. She saw Mr. Wilkins walk out, followed by a strange skinny man. She squinted her eyes to get a better look at the man. It took her a second, but she recognized him.

"Paul, that's Peter Jacobson!" Judy exclaimed.

"Who?" Paul asked.

"Peter Jacobson! The government secrets guy from the news! The one who's wanted!"

Judy remembered that there was a reward for any information on Peter Jacobson. She fumbled around her drawer and found a pen and notepad. They were getting into a car she didn't recognize, so she wrote down the license plate number so she could give it to the police.

"Judy, don't get Mr. Wilkins in trouble. He's been through enough."

"Oh, just shut up, Paul," Judy said as she picked up her phone and dialed 9-1-1.

***

Jeremiah and Peter pulled up to the isolated house on the outskirts of town. Peter had said that it was a few miles out, but he didn't say it was all the way out here. They had been driving for about 45 minutes, a lot of it through a bumpy dirt road. But Jeremiah understood the importance of not being somewhere where he could easily be found. Some part of Jeremiah's mind thought that being located in the middle of nowhere could be a little more conspicuous, but he put that thought aside.

Jeremiah stepped out of Peter's red 1999 Toyota Corolla and looked up at the house. It was a beige and green, modestly built, and not too big. From the outside it looked to be about two, maybe three, bedrooms and one story. There was nothing suspicious about it from the outside. You wouldn't know a fugitive was staying here.

Peter led the way to the front door without a word. Jeremiah noted that there was only one lock on this door. Something about that made Jeremiah chuckle inwardly, since he would've thought someone as paranoid as Peter would have something like ten locks on his front door. But then, that *would* look suspicious. Peter unlocked the door and motioned for Jeremiah to walk in first.

"I'm surprised you don't have some kind of security here, considering you're a wanted man."

"There's no point. No one knows I'm here, and if they did, this house is in the middle of a dirt lot. Not exactly the best of escape scenarios, even if I were in good health. I'd be caught almost immediately," Peter replied, as he flicked the lights to the living room on. He made a good point.

The house had a short and narrow hall from the doorway that led into the living room through a door of similar size to the front door. It was strange architecture, but it looked like it was meant to limit how many people could enter this house at one time. As he moved forward into the next room, Jeremiah wondered at the odds of finding such a conveniently built house in such a conveniently remote location.

Jeremiah looked into the living room, and every conspiracy theory movie he'd ever seen immediately rushed to his mind. This looked like a set for one of those movies, right down to the yarn connected between pictures of individuals. Next to that was a wall of newspaper clippings, most of which were of articles on the sudden changes in climate and the strange tide levels near the Pacific Ocean. What did any of that have to do with the Challenger Deep vessel?

"That's another strange little coincidence," Peter started, seeing Jeremiah reading the newspaper clippings, "You've noticed the dramatic shift in climate. How it's raining one day and full of sunshine the next. The tides are also rising at irregular levels, which is probably why the climate is changing the way it is. Can you guess when that started happening?"

Jeremiah took a shot in the dark, "A year and three months ago."

"Exactly. Like I said, there's something very strange going on here. Something big is being covered up. Every instinct I have is telling me that these events, as well as the complete lack of media coverage over the vessel being destroyed, are connected. And I want to blow the lid off of the whole thing. If I'm right, then the people deserve to know."

The evidence was there, Jeremiah had to admit. All signs pointed to a conspiracy, as ridiculous as it was to think that.

"Alright. What are you planning?" Jeremiah asked.

"Well, we need more information. So, we need to-" Peter was cut off by the sound of knocking at the front door.

"This is the police! Open up!" someone shouted from the other side of the door.

Peter's eyes widened at that sound, and he motioned for Jeremiah to stay quiet. Peter quietly made his way somewhere in the back of the house, leaving Jeremiah by himself in the living room. The knocking continued, as Jeremiah walked slowly through the door to the entrance hallway, unsure of what to do. Peter probably wasn't counting on this to happen, so he probably didn't have a contingency in case of this. Jeremiah was paralyzed and he had no idea where Peter had gone off to, or what he expected Jeremiah to do in this situation.

"Open the door before I kick it down!" The police officer yelled.

Jeremiah started to panic. Dealing with the police wasn't something he was exactly experienced with, but the longer he just stood there, the angrier the officer would get.

"Alright, you leave me no choice. I'm coming in!" The officer yelled. Three seconds later, the door sounded like it was kicked as hard as possible. Jeremiah watched as the hinges almost came off of the door frame before it was struck once more. This time, the door and its hinges came completely loose from the door frame and fell to the floor, revealing a young-looking police officer, no older than 25 or 26. He was dark haired, clean shaven, standing at about 6 feet tall and obviously in good shape. Stereotypical young hot shot, if Jeremiah had ever seen one.

The young police officer pulled his gun from its holster and aimed it at Jeremiah, "Put your hands on your head," he demanded.

Jeremiah finally found his voice, "You can't... you can't just kick in someone's door. Do you have a search warrant?"

"I told you to put your hands on your head!" the officer exclaimed.

Jeremiah complied with the officer's orders. The young cop then turned Jeremiah around and quickly placed handcuffs on his wrists, a task that was incredibly uncomfortable in this cramped hallway.

"Am I under arrest? What did I do?" Jeremiah asked, bewildered.

"Let's say, obstruction," he answered.

"Obstruction? I didn't do anything! I was just standing here!" Jeremiah exclaimed.

"You also didn't let me in. I have a warrant for the arrest of one Peter Jacobson, and I know for a fact that he's here. So, let's add harboring a fugitive to your list of offenses," the cop said. He then pointed Jeremiah down the hallway, "Walk," he demanded.

Jeremiah led the officer down the hallway, then stood to the side so the officer could walk into the living room.

"Stay right there, and don't try anything," the officer instructed.

He looked around and methodically searched the area. Jeremiah stood at the doorway to the living room, quietly observing as the young officer scanned every bit of the living room.

The police officer made his way to a doorway that looked like it led into a dining room of sorts. As soon as he crossed the threshold, Jeremiah watched as an iron pipe came down from the right side and crashed against the young police officer's skull with a loud *krraaak*. Jeremiah gasped in horror at that and rushed to the police officer's side.

"What the fuck!? I thought you were going to go hide, not bash a police officer over the head!" Jeremiah exclaimed, "What are we going to do now? What if he's dead?! That would make me an accomplice to murder! Oh shit, oh shit, oh shit!"

Jeremiah was pacing back and forth, muttering more panicked curses to himself. Peter gave Jeremiah a blank look before he swung his pipe and knocked him unconscious.

***

Jeremiah slowly came to, blinking his eyes open. He was sitting on the floor, his back leaning against a wall. The first thing he felt was a throbbing pain near his left temple. It took him a second to remember what had happened to him. Peter had hit a cop with an iron pipe, and then had done the same to Jeremiah. Angrily, he moved to stand up, but felt dizzy and had to support himself with the wall behind him. His eyesight was blurry and he couldn't quite focus. While he regained his faculties, he noticed that the handcuffs were no longer on his wrists. Peter must have taken them off of him while he was out.

"You woke up quickly. Good, I was afraid I did permanent damage. We have to get out of here," Peter said, somewhere to Jeremiah's left.

"What makes you think I'd help you after what you just did?" Jeremiah asked, angrily.

"Well, if you take a look at your ankle, I'm fairly certain you'll find the answer to that question."

Jeremiah looked down at his feet and saw a thick black band with a small box attached to it around his right ankle. It had a red beeping light on the black box portion of it. It looked like a bigger version of an ankle monitor worn by people on house arrest.

"An ankle monitor? How is an ankle monitor supposed to make me do what you say?"

"Well, for starters, that's not an ankle monitor. That's a small shrapnel bomb. And I have the switch for it right here," Peter said as he held up what looked like a TV remote with a small antenna attached to it, "So, you're going to keep helping me, or you're going to be a person shaped stain on the ground."

"But it's a bomb. If it goes off, you'll die too," Jeremiah said, convinced that Peter was bluffing.

"You would think so. But I have some clever friends who make bombs, and they made this one specifically for me. You see, when I press this button here," Peter said as he motioned to the switch, "The shrapnel in the bomb explodes out of the box in an upward direction. So, unless I'm standing on your shoulders, I'll be perfectly fine."

Jeremiah froze, realizing that he was stuck. He had no viable options here. It was either comply or get blown up, and that's not much of a choice.

"Let me get this straight. You know people who can run errands for you, rent a house for you, and make bombs for you. Why me? Why not any of your... your minions, or helpers?" Jeremiah asked.

"Because you care, Jeremiah. Because you *want* to know what happened. Anyone else, they wouldn't care. They'd just be doing what I say, they wouldn't have any real stake. You'll risk everything to know. I know you will. That bomb," Peter motioned to Jeremiah's ankle, "That's just a little insurance on the off chance that I'm wrong."

Jeremiah gritted his teeth, "Fine. What do we have to do?"

"Not we. You. And what you have to do, is break into a government building, plug me into their systems, and wait while I hack their database," Peter said, with a smug look on his face, "And we need to leave right now. This house isn't safe anymore."

Jeremiah reluctantly nodded his head before he got up from the floor and began following Peter when he made his way to the front door. Jeremiah paused for a second and looked around. All evidence of Peter's mania and obsession were gone. For someone who's supposedly sick, he did quick work of cleaning up after himself. Then, Jeremiah remembered something.

"Wait, what happened to the police officer?" Jeremiah asked.

"Don't worry about him." Peter replied.

Chapter 3

EARLIER. THE PACIFIC OCEAN.

"Captain Dennings," someone said.

Captain Roger Dennings turned around to see a young man he had recently hired to keep his boat clean while the rest of the crew did what they did best: fishing. They were currently the only boat out on the ocean, as fishermen were a very superstitious lot. The strange climate and tide behavior had scared everyone onto the land, but Captain Dennings didn't buy into any of that. He was here to fish and make money, and that's what he would do.

"Yes, Benny?"

"Well, sir, the entire boat is clean. There's not much left for me to do until we catch something. I was wondering if there was anything else you think I could do in the meantime," Benny said.

"Go see if anyone else needs a hand with their duties, tell them I sent you to help and they shouldn't give you too hard of a time."

Benny nodded and practically sprinted off to see how he could help. That was one overly ambitious kid. He was 19 years old and had apparently always had a fascination with the ocean, so he took the first job involving it that he could. He came from a poor family, or so he had said. He was a good kid, he did a good job on the boat. Maybe one day he'd be more than what's basically a janitor for the boat.

"Captain!" he heard James Tucker call. James Tucker was what most people would call the Captain's First Mate. He was in charge of most of the boat's operations and had an uncanny ability to predict which waters would be best for fishing. That's why Captain Dennings trusted him. He made the boat profitable.

"Yes, Tucker?"

"We've got something in the net, I'm bringing it up and dumping it on the deck. It feels heavy, Captain!" Tucker yelled.

Well, superstitions be damned, looks like this is going to be a good day to be out on these waters after all. All of his fellow captains would be eating their hearts out at the bar later.

Captain Dennings took a few steps back away from the deck to make room for their first catch of the day. He watched as his crew brought up the net they had cast about an hour prior. As soon as the net was above water, he saw that it was completely full to the brim with fish. This was a bigger haul than he'd ever had before! The net was then dropped right in front of the Captain, and as soon as it was, his nostrils were assaulted by the worst smell he'd ever experienced. Captain Dennings immediately raised his arm to cover his nose, hoping to escape the horrible stench of rotting corpses.

Once he'd recovered slightly from the assault on his sense of smell, he really paid attention to their catch. All of these fish were dead and had been for a while. Most of them were already rotted and fetid. This was all worthless. How the hell could this happen?

Captain Dennings looked up to see his entire crew watching in disbelief and covering their noses. None of them had ever seen something like this happen. Then again, neither had the Captain.

"Captain... look..." Benny said, just barely loud enough for the Captain to hear.

Captain Dennings looked up at Benny, who stood next to Tucker and the rest of the crew and saw them all looking out onto the ocean to their left. Captain Dennings looked to where their gaze was fixed and gasped in surprise. The ocean was barely visible anymore. The surface was covered in dead and rotting fish for about twenty feet in all directions, all looking as bad or worse than what they had just caught. The rotten smell of corpses was stronger than ever. Suddenly, Captain Dennings believed in superstition, and this was the worst omen they could have received out on the ocean.

"Captain," Tucker called, "What should we do?" Captain Dennings thought for a moment. This was unlike anything that has been reported on these waters. He had to go tell the authorities so they could look into what happened. There's no way all of these fish just spontaneously died for no reason. It could be an oil spill or some other kind of disaster that needed to be resolved quickly.

"We're going back to the port. We have to tell someone about this," said the Captain.

"What about all of these dead fish? Should we throw them back into the ocean?" asked Tucker.

"No, keep them on board. We'll show them to the authorities, so we don't sound like crazy people. This one is going to be a bit hard to swallow unless we show them proof. Tucker, turn the boat around, I can't stand smelling all of this death."

"Yes, Captain."

"And Benny," Captain Dennings started, getting the young boy's attention, "Do me a favor, use the phone outside of our bathroom and call the local authorities. Let them know we're on our way and that we found something very strange."

"Yes, Captain. No Problem sir," Benny said before running off to do as he was told.

Captain Dennings nodded his head and turned to look towards the ocean and all of these dead fish. Some of them, he didn't recognize as ever living close enough to the surface to be caught in one of their nets. They looked like deep-sea fish. His fellow captains might know something about this. Maybe they had some kind of legend about it and that's why they had all been so worried. Captain Dennings would ask them once they got back to port. For now, he just wanted to be out of this mess. It was depressing seeing his livelihood rotting away mere feet away from him.

***

"You're sure this is the spot?" he asked.

"Yup, this is where Cap'n Dennings docks his boat. He should be back soon, they phoned us about an hour ago. Surprised y'all made it down here so quickly," said the police officer.

"This kind of mess has to be cleaned up quickly. Thanks for letting us know, Officer Buckingham. Anyone else know about this?"

"Just the call center lady. But I told her it was someone fucking with us, so she's not a problem."

"Make sure of that, will you? You can go now."

"Mhmm," replied Officer Buckingham, before getting back into his run-down police cruiser. You'd think with being on the government's payroll for information, he'd be able to afford to drive something a little nicer.

Agent Craig looked around. This place was horribly unkempt. He could see the trash in the ocean not far from where he was standing. Every docking spot was in use except for one, which he presumed to belong to one Captain Dennings. These boats had seen better days, he could only imagine what their crews looked like.

Agent Craig heard cars pulling up behind him. He turned to see three black SUVs. Good, his clean-up crew was here. Everyone in the SUVs got out, five men per vehicle, wearing raincoats over their black pea jackets and black slacks. Agent Craig chuckled to himself. It looked like Agent Smith clones from The Matrix were arriving. He had never understood why the cleanup crew agents had to perpetuate the stereotype and dress the same. Meanwhile, Agent Craig wore blue jeans, a grey t-shirt and a green zip-up jacket. He could easily pass for a civilian, yet he was the one in charge of this little army of Agent Smiths. He'd always tried to keep his sense of humor about things. It was hard to do in his line of work.

Agent Craig turned back around to face the ocean and saw a little boat approaching. Well, this one at least looked cleaner than the rest of the ones that are docked here, but that's not saying much. As it got closer, Agent Craig couldn't help but plug his nose at the stench of rotting fish. Looks like they kept some of them aboard to show off. Wonderful. Agent Craig signaled for his clean-up crew to join him at the dock, right next to where Captain Dennings' boat was now being tied down.

A rugged looking man who seemed to be in his mid-30s or so climbed out of the boat and onto the dock. He was wearing stained overalls with a black long sleeve under it. He had a thick short beard on his face and his hairline was receding. Looks like he's probably the

Captain. The man stopped and looked at all of the agents behind Agent Craig, and then at Agent Craig suspiciously. Agent Craig smiled. He knew he didn't look like he was in charge of all of these men, so he decided to take the initiative and stepped forward with a hand extended.

"Captain Dennings?"

The man took Agent Craig's hand and shook it firmly, "That's me. And you are?"

"I'm the man in charge. My men and I are here to get some information and clean up the mess."

Captain Dennings furrowed his brow, "They sent feds to clean up a section of the ocean?"

"Something like that. Do you mind if some of my men board your boat to get a look at what you brought us?"

"Well, seems I don't have much of a choice. Go ahead," Captain Dennings said, obviously unhappy about having strangers on his boat.

Agent Craig nodded his head at his men, and eight of them made their way onto the boat. They immediately flinched at the smell of the rotten fish on the ship. The top deck of the boat was slightly more elevated than the dock, so anyone boarding would have to step up onto it and anyone leaving would have to carefully step down.

The floor of the deck was covered in the innards of the rotten fish, making it quite slippery. It'd be difficult to leave the boat in a hurry.

"So, fishing in the evening, huh?" Agent Craig asked.

"Water's traditionally calmer once the sun sets. Not so much these days, but old habits die hard."

"Indeed, they do."

"So, why's a government agent taking care of a local fish issue?" Captain Dennings asked as he moved to stand next to Agent Craig and looked at Craig's men on his boat.

"Let's just say it's in my boss's best interest to get things like this taken care of as soon as possible."

"Interesting. He some kind of environmentalist or something?"

Agent Craig smirked as he watched his men give the signal that they were ready, "Or something."

Agent Craig snapped his fingers twice, giving his men the go ahead. Almost immediately, they all drew silenced 9mm pistols, and quickly dispatched Captain Denning's entire crew. From the sound of it, there seemed to have been 8 men in total. Agent Craig turned his head to look at Captain Dennings, his face frozen in horror at the sight of his men being killed right in front of him. Agent Craig drew his own silenced 9mm and pointed it at Captain Dennings' head.

Captain Dennings looked like he was about to open his mouth and say something or ask something, but Agent Craig wasn't interested, so he pulled the trigger and killed him before he could get a word out. He didn't want to deal with any inane questions about why they're doing this, as if the answer would change anything.

Agent Craig turned to see his other seven men still standing behind him, "Alright guys, it's time to make all of this nastiness go away. Get rid of the bodies, clean up the dock, close off the area, take the boat out to where they reported seeing all the dead fish, and clean it all up. I'll feed a story about a local boat being brought down by an unexpected wave with no survivors to the press. We'll probably smash up the boat as the final nail in the coffin. Let's get to work," Agent Craig was interrupted by the sound of his phone ringing.

He reached into his jeans pocket and grabbed his black cell phone. He checked who was calling before touching ANSWER on the screen, "Agent Craig, here."

"We got a call from one of our informants. A few hours north of your position, there's a reported sighting of Mr. Jacobson."

"Ah. The whistleblower finally slipped up and got seen," Agent Craig replied.

"There's an APB out on the license plate numbers seen on the car he was driving. We need you up there to make sure he doesn't talk. We don't know what he's learned since he's been on the loose."

"Yeah, I got it. Just send me a message telling me where I'm going."

"Remember, quick and quiet."

"Got it, thanks," Agent Craig said.

Agent Craig touched the icon to hang up on his phone and put it back in his pocket. He turned back around to look at his clean-up crew, "Alright guys, I have to go take care of another loose end. Get it done."

He didn't wait for them to answer. It'd only be a matter of time before the cops made a dumb move and let Mr. Jacobson know they know where he is. He had to get there before that happened.

***

Agent Craig loved driving fast. In that situation, he had no time to let his mind wander. It wasn't possible for him to become distracted. All of his attention was focused on the road and weaving in and out of traffic, at once relaxing and exhilarating. It cleared his mind but also sharpened it. His superiors didn't necessarily know about this particular proclivity of his, so they assumed that it would take him longer to catch up to the whistleblower. It would have taken anyone obeying traffic laws about two and a half hours to three hours get to his destination, but after only two hours had passed, Agent Craig was almost there. He'd thought of suggesting the code name "Speed Demon," but then he remembered that everyone he works with is much more serious about things than he is.

On his way there, Agent Craig had received a message telling him exactly where they had found Mr. Jacobson's car parked. It was an isolated house in the middle of nowhere. The outskirts. Could he have found a more stereotypical place to hide?

Craig grimaced as his car started bumping through the dirt road that would lead him to the isolated house. He would have to get his car washed after this, and he hated what dirt roads did to his suspension. Agent Craig thought to himself that he would deal with the whistleblower in proportion to how dirty his car got on the way to him. The dirtier the car, the more he'd beat him before taking him in. He'd just tell his superiors that one of the cops in town did that to him, which would be easy to believe. Hotshot cops itching to prove themselves are a dime a dozen around here.

After a few minutes of that dreadful dirt road, Agent Craig pulled up to the house in the middle of nowhere. Agent Craig chuckled to himself at that thought, thinking that it would make a great horror movie title. A bit derivative, but what wasn't these days?

Agent Craig got out of his vehicle and looked around. There were no lights on in the house and the only other car parked here was a police cruiser. He sighed at the realization that it seemed he was right, and some local cop had tipped Mr. Jacobson off and he had made his escape before Agent Craig could get here.

"Damn you, local law enforcement," Agent Craig whispered to himself.

Agent Craig decided to go in and take a look. If Mr. Jacobson was getting sloppy enough to let someone see him drive off, maybe he was getting sloppy enough to leave behind a clue as to his whereabouts.

The front door was unlocked, meaning he probably left in a hurry. Agent Craig walked inside and flicked the light switch by the door on, illuminating the hallway leading into what looked like the living room. He made his way through, careful to listen for any sounds, and flicked the light on in the living room.

Unfortunately, there was nothing here to go off of. He saw some tacks pressed into a blank board on one wall, giving the suggestion of a clue, but it looks like whatever was here was taken down when Mr. Jacobson vacated the premises. Looked like he wasn't getting as sloppy as Agent Craig had hoped.

"Hello? Is someone up there?"

Agent Craig turned around at the sound of someone's voice. He saw an open doorway leading to a dark basement. *Stop me if you've heard this one before*, Agent Craig thought to himself. He drew the gun from the holster under his jacket and cocked it, just in case.

He carefully walked down the stairs, while listening to what sounded like someone struggling against a restraint.

Agent Craig reached the bottom of the stairs, where the room was pitch black. He felt around the wall to the left of him for a light switch but found none. When he felt around the wall to his right, he found it and flicked it on.

The basement was empty, save for a washer and dryer, a water heater, and a police officer with blood running down the side of his face. So, all in all, fairly tame for the basement of a crazy person.

"Thank God! That lunatic Peter Jacobson hit me in the head with a fucking pipe and tied me up! Untie me!"

Agent Craig lowered his gun to his side and rolled his eyes at the incompetent cop.

"How long ago did he leave?" Agent Craig asked.

"Fuck, I don't know. I think they were already gone when I woke up like ten minutes ago. I haven't heard anything from upstairs since you got here."

"Did you say 'they'?"

"Yeah, there was some man with that Jacobson guy," the cop said.

"What did he look like?" Agent Craig asked.

"Uh... middle aged, physically fit, tall? Can you just untie me?"

Agent Craig ignored the cop's request. He turned around, pulled out his phone, and called his superiors.

"Craig here. I found his old hideout. He seems to have left a few minutes before I got here. I might be able to catch him. There also seems to be another person with him."

"Hurry, then. This is important."

"I know. One more thing, Mr. Jacobson killed a police officer," Agent Craig said.

"Wait, what?!" the cop exclaimed when he heard that.

"We'll send someone out there to clean up the mess. Get on with it, Craig."

"Understood," Agent Craig said before he hung up.

Agent Craig raised his gun and aimed it at the police officer's head.

"Come on man, you don't have to-"

The cop didn't get a chance to finish his sentence before Agent Craig pulled the trigger and killed him. Can't have any loose ends. Quickly and quietly, that was the order. Can't exactly have it be quiet if there's some cop having water cooler conversations he shouldn't. Agent Craig exited the house, turning off all the lights as he went and leaving everything as it was. The clean-up crew would take care of all of this.

Outside, Agent Craig retrieved a flashlight from his vehicle and searched around the perimeter. He saw a pair of tire tracks leading further away from town, still on the dirt road. He grimaced, knowing he'd have to dirty his car some more to catch up to them. Mr. Jacobson's going to pay for every single scuff. He got into his car, turned it on, and started following the tire tracks.

***

They were here again. It was a little hard to miss the signs. At least, it was hard for Jana to miss them. No one else seemed to notice the erratic behavior. Everyone just thought that it was for entertainment purposes.

Such is life working at SeaWorld.

Jana's lifelong adoration of undersea life hadn't culminated in the prestigious field of marine biology like she had expected it would. Due to her crippling social anxiety and unwavering paranoia, Jana hadn't been able to accomplish a whole lot. At least that was how she rationalized her failures in her head. It made it easier to make peace with the fact that instead of studying undersea life like she had planned, she found herself in the business of oceanic entertainment.

Despite all of that, her keen abilities of observation had not left her, and she was able to note the differences in the behavior of most of the aquatic animals that signaled something was wrong. Their swimming patterns were somehow different, as if they were looking for something. It resembled anticipation.

As she watched, the fish all changed direction. In unison, they all seemed to point themselves in the direction of one person. Not too far from her, she saw someone in a dark grey hoodie put their hand up against the glass of one of the tanks. And, as if this person were calling out to them, all of the fish in the tank moved towards where this stranger's hand was placed.

Jana watched, half in awe and half in curiosity. It was only as the stranger withdrew their hand that she noticed there was something strange about their skin. It reminded her of something else, and she strained trying to remember.

A moment later, she remembered.

The face in the glass, she thought to herself. The skin on that hand reminded her of the face she saw in the glass at the grocery store. But once again, it was gone too quickly to get a good look at it.

Either way, this time she was positive. This time she knew that she had seen something strange. She wasn't being plagued by paranoia this time. Someone or something was following her, and now she had proof. She just had to follow this stranger.

Abandoning her duties, Jana powerwalked as inconspicuously as she could. She, at once, felt courageous and petrified. Attempting to confront something that she feared was not in her repertoire of special skills, but she knew that if she didn't do something, she may never get another chance.

Unfortunately, SeaWorld is not an empty place that can be traversed quickly whilst tailing someone, and it wasn't long before the relentless foot traffic gave her pursuit the necessary openings to escape her line of sight.

So, there she stood, having failed in her objective. But at least now she knew beyond a shadow of a doubt.

Something is coming for me.

Chapter 4

Peter stopped the car near a big fenced off area with a building that looked like some kind of hangar in the middle. Jeremiah wondered if this strange little adventure of his would ever run out of political thriller clichés. They had been driving for about an hour, never once actually getting on a road. Peter had said that he didn't want to risk getting the cops called on them again. Jeremiah had chuckled at the hilarity of going off road to not get in trouble with the cops.

"Alright, so what now?" Jeremiah asked.

"Now, you sneak into that building, find a computer, turn it on, and plug this in," Peter said as he handed Jeremiah a very small looking USB flash drive.

"I'm going to assume this isn't a flash drive."

"You're not an idiot. Of course it isn't. It'll let me remotely access that computer from the car with my laptop. I'll be able to look for whatever we need to blow the lid off of this conspiracy. Maybe the biggest one since Roswell," Peter said, practically foaming at the mouth.

"It's creepy how much you're enjoying this," Jeremiah said under his breath, but loud enough for Peter to hear.

Peter shot him a serious look, "Just get in there and get it done. And don't forget," Peter lifted and waved the remote to Jeremiah's bomb, "Your life is in my hands."

"What? No walkie-talkie or anything?"

Peter silently slid what looked like a small Bluetooth headset to Jeremiah. Jeremiah put it in his ear, and heard Peter's voice in his ear say, "Good enough for you?" Jeremiah gave Peter a thumbs up, though admittedly, it wasn't the finger he was dying to show him.

Jeremiah got out of the car and walked up to the tall fence in front of him. He knew he was in good shape, but he was no acrobat and would have to be careful climbing this. Luckily, there didn't seem to be any barbed wire or extra security at the top of this fence.

He regretted not asking for gloves as his hands gripped the chain link fence and he began climbing. After what seemed like an eternity, he was at the top.

He swung his legs over to the other side and climbed about halfway down before deciding to save some time by letting go and landing on his feet.

"I can't believe I didn't ask this before, but what if I run into anyone in there? What do I do?" Jeremiah asked.

"I wouldn't worry about that. This building hasn't been in use for about two years. I've done my homework on this. I wouldn't send you in if I thought there was a chance you'd fail. We both only have one shot at this."

Jeremiah continued walking towards the building and had another thought, "Then why do you think there will still be a computer for me to turn on in there?"

"I may or may not have pried the information out of someone who has actually been in there," Peter said.

"If you know someone who could get in there, why not ask them to do this?"

"Because I wasn't able to strap a bomb to *their* ankle," Peter replied.

"Why couldn't you hack into... whatever you're going to hack into from a regular computer?" Jeremiah asked.

"Because this one has a wireless router installed on it that's built for accessing the government and military databases. Do you know of a regular computer that has that installed?" Peter asked sarcastically.

"No. But, why would they leave something like this just lying around?" Jeremiah asked.

"They didn't. Someone else brought it into the building afterwards. Our little 'infiltration' isn't the first shady thing to happen here, we're just taking advantage of the previous 'mastermind's' clumsiness." Peter replied.

"Alright, then."

After a few minutes at a brisk pace, Jeremiah was at the building. He walked around the building, looking for an opening to get inside. The doors were all locked tight, but he eventually came across a window large enough for him to climb through and that he could break. He fumbled around the floor, looking for a rock or something similarly hard to break the window with. He finally found a stone bigger than his fist a few feet away from the window. *How convenient.*

He made sure he was a few feet away from the window and threw the stone as hard as he could. It hit with a loud crack, the window not completely broken, but the glass would give way with one more throw of the stone. Jeremiah did so, and the stone fell through the now shattered window. Jeremiah carefully cleared the rest of the glass from the windowsill before attempting to climb through.

Quite ungracefully, Jeremiah crawled through the opening and almost lost his balance when entering the building. Once he regained his composure, he let Peter know that he was now inside.

"Good. Look for that computer. Quickly."

You don't have to tell me twice, Jeremiah thought. The inside of this building looked pretty creepy. Luckily, the computer itself was easy to spot. It sat on a desk on the opposite side of where he entered. There wasn't much else in the building. Some scrap metal in the corners, locks on all of the doors, and some random pieces of tech strewn about. It looked like they were unimportant and left behind for that very reason.

Jeremiah quickly made his way to the computer which consisted of an old looking monitor attached to a bulky computer tower. He said this place hadn't been used for two years, but this computer looked much older than that. He traced the power cord behind the tower and found that it was plugged into a small generator sitting behind the desk, hidden from view. Jeremiah found the switch to turn the generator on and flicked it. The generator didn't turn on, and Jeremiah wondered why he thought it would be that easy.

"What's taking so long?" Peter asked, obviously anxious.

"I have to get this generator going. Hang on."

Jeremiah pulled the generator from behind the desk, careful not to unplug the computer tower from it, and found a cord used to rev up the generator and give it some juice. He turned the power switch off and pulled the cord several times until he saw a light next to the power switch turn green. He then flicked the switch once more and the generator turned on.

Jeremiah then moved back to the computer tower and pressed the power button. The computer monitor lit up and the machine began to boot up, rather slowly.

"The computer is turning on," Jeremiah said.

"Good. As soon as it finishes booting up, just plug in the USB device I gave you, and I'll take it from there."

"Am I leaving once it's plugged in?" Jeremiah asked.

"Of course not. You have to bring the USB device back. We can't leave anything that can be traced to me here. Are you insane?" Peter asked.

"I'm starting to think so," Jeremiah muttered.

Jeremiah waited until the computer had finished booting up. It didn't look like any OS that he had seen before, it was a plain black screen with green text, much like a BIOS screen on a normal computer, but with fewer options available. Jeremiah looked for a USB port on the computer tower, finally finding a single port in the back.

"Alright, I'm plugging in the USB device," Jeremiah said.

He plugged it in and stood back to look at the monitor. He watched as Peter remotely input a series of commands he didn't understand. Computers had never really been his strong suit, and none of what he was seeing made any sense.

"Seeing anything pertinent yet?" Jeremiah asked.

"Quiet!" Peter exclaimed.

Jeremiah rolled his eyes and continued to watch the monitor, waiting for Peter to tell him he could get out of this creepy building. As he watched, he glimpsed something that immediately caught his attention. "Sasha Wilkins."

"Wait, wait, wait, go back. I saw my wife's name!" Jeremiah said quickly.

"I know. Just wait, I'm collecting all the data. We'll look at it once we're out of here."

Dammit! Jeremiah thought. The truth about what happened to his wife could be so close. He could finally know what went wrong.

After a few more minutes of indecipherable computer inputs, Peter finally spoke up, "Alright. Grab the USB device and destroy the computer tower."

"Sure, because there's tons of things to use to break a computer tower around here," Jeremiah replied.

"You sure don't talk to me like I can decide to kill you at any moment."

Jeremiah gritted his teeth and complied with Peter's wishes. He unplugged the device, put it in his pocket, and looked around. All he could use was the rock on the ground from his break in. He jogged over to it, picked it up, and returned to the computer. He quickly bashed the case open and used the rock to break everything inside of it. The circuits sparked against the rock, making Jeremiah temporarily afraid that he might start a fire. Fortunately, that didn't happen and everything just broke.

"Consider it destroyed," Jeremiah said.

"Good. Now get back to the car," Peter replied.

Jeremiah walked back to the broken window and carefully climbed through to the other side. This time, he did lose his balance and fall to the ground. Thankfully, there was no broken glass on this side of the window. The suspense of finally learning the truth was making Jeremiah clumsy. He jogged back to the fence, eager to see what Peter had uncovered.

This time, Jeremiah threw caution to the wind and climbed the fence as fast as he could, ignoring the biting pain in his hands as he did so. At the top, he didn't climb down at all, he simply jumped to save time. He briskly walked to the car, opened the passenger door and got inside.

"Good job," Peter said as Jeremiah sat down.

"What did you get?" Jeremiah asked.

Peter gave Jeremiah a sly smirk, "Everything."

Chapter 5

That was ominous.

"Everything? What does that mean?" Jeremiah asked.

"Well, I'm still reading through the files, but... this looks like exactly what we were looking for. There are logs from the vessel and communications sent back and forth."

"Let's read them, then!" Jeremiah exclaimed.

Peter gave him a blank look, "We're not going to read them here. We have to get somewhere safe so we can really take a good look at everything and finally piece together this puzzle," Peter said.

"Alright, fine. Let's go," Jeremiah replied.

Peter turned the ignition and the car roared to life. He quickly shifted into drive and began heading in the opposite direction they had come from.

"You seem like you're a very careful person," Jeremiah said.

"Well, I have to be. I'm wanted by the government of the country I live in. What's your point?" Peter asked.

"Well, for someone who's so careful, why did you not know what to do when the police showed up at your hideout?"

Peter sighed before answering, "I didn't think that would ever happen. I plan all of my moves, prepare contingencies, and have back up plans for anything that could go wrong. But, I'm always so careful, I didn't think the police would ever find me. And we weren't going to be there long. I expected us to be in and out before it mattered anyway. I... I slipped, I suppose."

"Let's hope you don't slip again..." Jeremiah replied.

Jeremiah sat in silence as Peter drove. He couldn't help but let his mind wander at what could possibly be in those files they had just recovered. He wondered at what his wife's final thoughts may have been while at the bottom of the ocean. He was anxious to finally learn the truth, but he understood that getting somewhere they wouldn't be found was a priority. As much as he resented it, he needed Peter so he could finally know everything.

"Now that we have what we were after," Jeremiah started, "Is there any way you could remove this bomb from my ankle?"

Peter didn't even look at him as he answered, "While I'd love to trust you, it's hard to imagine you don't harbor some negative feelings towards me. Who's to say you wouldn't attack me the second I lose my leverage over you?"

"I wouldn't. I need you and the information you have," Jeremiah replied.

"Even so, I don't want to take any more risks. Especially not when we've gotten this far. Once this whole thing is over, I'll remove it. But until then, your life is collateral for your cooperation."

Jeremiah sighed in frustration. Normal people aren't this paranoid, but Peter made his living looking over his shoulder while exposing secrets. He wouldn't have gotten as far as he has without an unhealthy amount of paranoia.

"Back at my house... you said that you're sick," Jeremiah said.

"Nothing gets by you, does it?" Peter replied.

"How sick are you?" Jeremiah asked.

"Sick enough that we're on a time crunch. Sick enough that I need someone like you to help me. Sick enough that this will be the last secret I uncover." Peter said sternly.

"Is that why you're so obsessed with it?"

"Tell me something, Jerry," Jeremiah scowled at Peter's use of that nickname, "if I told you that you were going to die in a month, wouldn't you use that month to leave behind some kind of legacy for yourself? Or would you let your name fade into obscurity? I intend to go out with a bang. And something like this is the biggest one I could go out on. So yes, that is why I'm so obsessed. Frankly, I'm shocked you aren't, your wife having died because of this, and all."

"We still don't know any of the details," Jeremiah replied quietly.

"We will, soon."

***

Agent Craig followed the tire tracks until he reached an old and unused military facility behind a fence. If Agent Craig's suspicions were correct, these two yahoos just used an old military computer to get their hands on some files his superiors don't want them to have. He grabbed his phone from his pocket and called a friend he had in intelligence.

"Hello?" answered a voice after a few seconds.

"Rodney, it's Craig."

"What do you want?" Rodney asked in a hostile tone.

"Whoa, what's with the third degree, bud?"

"You have a lot of nerve, Craig. Calling me and being so casual," Rodney said.

"Come on, Rod. It's been three years, haven't you forgiven me yet?" Craig asked wryly.

"No. No, I haven't. And don't call me that," Rodney said stoically.

"Fine, fine, fine. I'm sorry, alright? But I'm calling about something important. I need to know if there's recently been any access to the military servers from Hangar 729. Can you help me out?"

There were a few seconds of silence from the other line before Agent Craig finally heard a deep sigh and the clicking of keys. After a few moments, Rodney answered.

"Looks like someone logged into the servers about twenty minutes ago. But from what I can see, they didn't really do anything. It looks like they logged in, stayed logged in for five minutes, then logged out."

"Is there any way they deleted their traces?"

"I don't know of anyone who could do something like that with our servers. But I can run a scan and see if there's any activity that's been erased," Rodney replied.

"Please, do."

A few more minutes of silence later, Craig heard Rodney sigh.

"What is it?" Agent Craig asked.

"Well, you were right. The five minutes of activity in between the log in and the log out have been erased completely from the servers. It didn't set off any alarms. I tried to find out what was accessed, but it's behind a wall of encryption that even I don't have access to."

"Shit. That's what I was afraid of. Thank you, Rodney. This was a big help."

Just as Agent Craig was about to hang up, he heard Rodney, "Wait, Craig."

"Yes?"

"I hate you," Rodney started, "But... I miss you. And... I still love you."

Agent Craig paused for a moment, trying to figure out exactly what to say, "I know, Rodney. Look, once I'm done with my current assignment... We can get together and talk."

"Are you lying to me again?" Rodney asked.

Agent Craig looked at the ground and saw where the tire tracks continued past the facility, "I hope not."

Agent Craig hung up the phone and got back in his car. He started the engine and gunned it in the direction the tracks headed. Wherever they were going, he would catch them this time even with Rodney's confession weighing on Agent Craig as he drove. He and Rodney had a complicated past. He had to get it out of his mind and focus on the assignment. It was imperative that he find Mr. Jacobson and his accomplice before they revealed anything to the public. He would think about Rodney once that was done.

**

After an hour of driving, and Peter and Jeremiah were near their destination. They had driven through a forest to arrive at a lone cabin in the thick of it. *We've reached the horror movie section of our journey, Mr. Wilkins,* Jeremiah thought to himself as they parked and got out of the car. They had parked a little out of the way of the cabin, so they had some walking to do now.

"Just how many of these hidey-holes do you have?" Jeremiah asked.

"Not enough, if you ask me," Peter replied.

They walked up to the front door of the cabin. It looked like one of those log cabins you'd see when you looked up photos of Abraham Lincoln, complete with a porch and a rocking chair. No one would expect this to be the hiding place of someone like Peter Jacobson. They would suspect it's the hiding place of a serial killer, maybe, but not a government whistleblower.

Peter fumbled with the keys in his hands before he entered a coughing fit and dropped them on the porch they stood on. Jeremiah bent down to pick up the keys, and when he did, Peter shoved him back and raised up the remote to the bomb threateningly.

"Calm down, I was just trying to help," Jeremiah said, with his hands raised, as if surrendering.

Peter tried to regain his composure, but he kept letting out small coughs here and there, rendering him almost unable to reply. He kneeled down and picked the keys up himself, unlocked the door, and let both of them inside of the cabin. Once inside, Peter turned on the lights, and Jeremiah saw that it was a lot smaller on the inside. The size of the average living room, there were two cots, a makeshift kitchen, a port-o-potty, and a desk with a high-tech looking computer situated on it that stuck out like a sore thumb. Peter locked the door behind them, still letting out strained coughs between each breath.

"I know that cough, Peter. You have lung cancer," Jeremiah stated plainly.

Peter looked at him and nodded somberly.

"My father died of lung cancer a couple of years after my wife left. I spent some time taking care of him before he... succumbed. I couldn't forget that cough if I wanted to."

Peter didn't respond to that as he moved towards the computer and turned it on. He stood there, with his back turned to Jeremiah for a full minute, most likely trying to ground himself and calm his breathing. Finally, he turned around and faced Jeremiah.

"Are you ready to learn what happened to your wife?"

***

Half an hour later, and Jeremiah and Peter stared at the computer monitor. Neither was able to say anything, both men in shock at what they had just learned. Finally, Jeremiah spoke up, "This can't be real... can it?"

"Apparently, it is," Peter responded.

"How could this have gone undetected for ten years? How could they have replaced most of the crew without anyone noticing anything was off?"

"I don't know, Jeremiah!" Peter exclaimed, "It says that the crew that went on the mission was the same crew that signed on for it months prior. Whatever happened, whoever took their place, no one noticed."

"My wife would've noticed," Jeremiah said, "She had met one of them before. Albert, the lead engineer. She had met him months before the voyage!"

"Then... I don't know. The imposters must have looked like the people they replaced."

"How is that even possible?" Jeremiah asked.

"I don't know!"

"Let's go through what we do know, then," Jeremiah said.

"Alright. What we do know is that most of the crew onboard the vessel were imposters. They sent a transmission to the real crew's superiors at the end of their voyage declaring themselves as such, probably right at the end. The transcription is still on the screen," Peter said.

Jeremiah went to read it again, still trying to process what they just learned.

This mission has been compromised. We are the Children of the Sea,and we have been in control of this voyage since the beginning.The real crew of this voyage is dead. You'll find their bodies atthe provided coordinates. We did this for our greater purpose.Humanity cannot continue thinking they are the true heirs of theplanet. On this day, our plans to awaken the true children of God cometo fruition. We needed your vessel, your scientists and your funding to finally accomplish this. Today is the beginning of the end. And we arehappily giving our lives for this. We will be the first sacrifices to Them.And we have you to thank. They will inherit the earth. The Great Sea Gods.

Jeremiah read it over and over again. This is not what he had expected to learn. His wife had died because of some religious fanatics hijacking a government voyage. He couldn't believe it. He didn't want to believe it.

"What are the odds that this is fake, and we're being taken for a ride?" Jeremiah asked.

"I know this is hard to swallow, trust me. I don't believe it myself and uncovering secrets is what I do. But this is real. It wouldn't have been so well hidden and encrypted if it was fake," Peter replied.

"So, then... that means these people, the 'Children of the Sea,' woke something up at the bottom of the ocean? Then why haven't we seen anything yet? It's been over a year," Jeremiah said.

"Probably for the same reason it took the vessel 10 years to reach the bottom of the ocean. Whatever these things are, they're rising slowly, I think. But this explains the strange things happening in the Pacific Ocean. The strange tidal activity, the erratic weather around the western US... it all fits," Peter said.

"Why is this being kept a secret from the public? Don't they think we deserve to know if there's something coming to... to kill us? Or whatever it is they're going to do?" Jeremiah asked.

Peter turned his attention back to the computer and looked through some more of the files they had gotten for a minute before answering, "Something about not wanting to start a panic. And that there's a plan, but no mention of what the plan actually is. And... huh."

"What is it?" Jeremiah asked.

"From what I can gather, it looks like very few people actually know about what's going on. I found an access log, and there's less than twenty names on this list. If this is accurate, then not even the president knows about it. A couple of military personnel, a few congressmen, and some names even I don't recognize. This... This is bigger than I thought. This is bigger than I ever imagined," Peter said.

"I still can't believe this. This is all too... unreal."

"We'd better start believing," Peter replied.

"Alright. Let's say this is real, and there is... something... rising from the bottom of the ocean to, uh, 'Inherit the earth.' What do we do?" Jeremiah asked.

At that moment, the door to the cabin swung open, revealing a man wearing jeans and a green jacket, pointing a gun directly at Peter.

"This is the part where you both surrender and come with me," said Agent Craig.

***

Another day, another dollar, Jana thought as she parked her car. She wasn't terribly excited to be going to work, but one must do what one must. She hadn't been sleeping well since she was confronted with proof that she's not just a paranoid mess. One would think that confirmation that suspicions held were rational would have a more positive effect on the psyche, but one would be very incorrect in thinking that. If anything, that confirmation did nothing but make Jana even more of a paranoid mess than she had already been.

Whoever or whatever was following her had shown up in two places that she frequented. It wasn't a stretch to think that they knew where she lived as well. Jana had added another two locks to her already comical looking door. But adding them didn't really make her feel any better. If anything, it just felt like another small hurdle they'd need to go over if they really wanted to get her. Jana really hoped that they didn't want to get her.

With all of the motivation she could muster, Jana got out of her car and walked slowly towards the entrance to work. When she first started working here, she was going in through the main entrance like all of the people visiting the park did. It's amazing how red Jana can get when she's embarrassed, a fact that she learned two weeks into her employment when her supervisor informed her that employees have their own entrance near the back of the park. Reliving that memory, she made her way there, avoiding eye contact with any of the park visitors, lest they be one of *them.*

Keeping your head down is a really good way to not notice what's in front of you. At least not until it's directly in your path. Because of this fact, Jana didn't see that someone was standing in front of the employee entrance until they entered her field of vision that was focused on the ground in front of her.

A muddy pair of black boots. That's the first thing she noticed. As her eyes moved up from there, her fear only increased. Her gaze was greeted by brown pants, and a plain black shirt covered by a green coat, all of which were muddy. When her eyes finally met the face that belonged to this figure, her breath caught in her throat. He looked... *drowned.*

His face looked like he'd been in water for too long. As if he'd been there for his entire life. It was hard to look at, and yet she couldn't look away. She was paralyzed with fear, yet his eyes looked both serious and calm. It was then that she truly took note of how large this man was. There was no doubt in Jana's mind that this was the end of her if he wanted it to be.

It could've been seconds, or it could've been hours, but eventually the man turned towards the parking lot and walked away. Jana couldn't do or say anything. She was still stunned, with bit of her paranoia and anxiety taking full control of her. All she could do was stand there, mouth agape, and wait for it to pass. Once it did, she let out a breath she was very sure she'd been holding for longer than what was healthy. That's when her mind began to race with questions she had no answers for.

Why hadn't he said anything? If he was following her, and it wasn't to corner her and take her somewhere, then why? If he wanted something from her, or simply to *do* something to her, then this was the perfect opportunity. But he said nothing and just walked away.

Why?

With questions burning in her mind, Jana forced her shaky legs to carry her forward through the employee entrance. She had a face to associate with her fears now. But she had no idea now what they wanted any more than she had when she woke up this morning. The who may no longer be completely unknown, but so many other questions remained. Questions that she would no doubt spend all day obsessing over. She needed help. And she needed it sooner rather than later.

BRIAN MELGAR

<u>Chapter 6</u>

Peter and Jeremiah immediately put their hands up in surrender, looking at the man who had just silently picked the lock on the cabin door.

"Who.. who are you?" Jeremiah stuttered.

"Yeah, I'm going to go ahead and not tell you, and just say that you're under arrest and are coming with me," Agent Craig replied.

"Under arrest? Are you a cop?" Peter asked, looking the man up and down, "You're not dressed like a cop."

"I'm not a cop, but you're going to want to listen to me anyway. Now just step away from the computer and come with me. And you," Agent Craig pointed at Peter, "are going to be very upset that I had to go through so much trouble to find you."

"Wait, wait, wait!" Jeremiah exclaimed as he walked forward a bit, causing Agent Craig to aim his gun at him instead. Jeremiah paused.

"Just... hold on a second. Do you have any idea what we just found?" Jeremiah asked.

"All I know is you weren't supposed to find it. I don't really care what it was."

"You should care! This... this is huge!" Jeremiah exclaimed.

Agent Craig kept his gun trained on Jeremiah and his eyes shifted between him and Peter. He was slightly considering what they were saying. Agent Craig wasn't one to go against his orders, he'd always been loyal to his government and their wishes. But they'd never wanted Peter Jacobson taken care of this badly. He'd uncovered plenty of things in the last twenty years, why was it that this particular secret was so important?

"You," Agent Craig said, looking at Jeremiah, "Find something to tie Mr. Jacobson up with. I don't want to take any risks."

"What am I supposed to tie him up with?" Jeremiah asked.

"I don't care. Just do it."

Jeremiah looked around the cabin, looking for something to use to comply with this man's wishes. All he saw were the blankets for the cots. He walked over to his cot and grabbed the blanket.

"Is this fine?" Jeremiah asked.

"Yes, yes, yes. Just hurry and tie him up," Agent Craig replied hastily.

Jeremiah walked over to Peter, the man's gun still trained on him, now with both of them in his sights. He wrapped the blanket around Peter below his shoulders, folded enough that it only covered his upper arms. He tied it at his back, taking care not to put too much pressure around Peter's chest.

"Make sure it's tight, or you both get an unnecessary bullet before I take you in," Agent Craig said.

Jeremiah complied and tied the blanket tighter around Peter. He heard him stifle a cough and felt a tinge of remorse for having to do this. Once he was done, he turned to face the man with his hands raised, standing next to Peter.

"What's your name?" Agent Craig asked.

"Jeremiah Wilkins."

"Alright," Agent Craig said, right before shooting Jeremiah in the left thigh, "You can call me Craig."

Jeremiah fell to the ground and yelled in extreme pain, clutching at his leg. The bullet wound was pouring blood onto the cabin floor.

"Don't be such a drama queen. The bullet didn't even hit a bone. It went through clean, it's even behind you on the floor. You'll be fine. But, you know, keep some pressure on it. Just in case," Agent Craig said.

Peter looked shocked, and as if he was about to advance on Craig.

"I would sit down if I were you, Mr. Jacobson," Craig said as he raised his gun to aim at Peter, "Unless you want me to *make* you sit, like your friend there."

Peter reluctantly complied and used the wall behind him to slide down to a sitting position. Once he was there, Craig lowered his gun and walked over to the computer to take a look at whatever it is they thought was so important. Soon, the screen had his full attention.

"Are you alright?" Peter asked.

"No, I'm not alright, he shot me!" Jeremiah replied.

"I know, I know. Listen. The.. the thing, on your ankle. It has a release button. At the bottom of the box. If you hold it down for five seconds, it comes off," Peter whispered.

Jeremiah looked at Peter, and saw him reaching into his pocket. He still had the remote to the bomb. He wanted them to use the bomb to take out Craig and get away. Jeremiah gave Peter a panicked expression, letting him know that he didn't want to do this.

"We can't trust him," Peter whispered, "We don't know that he'll listen. We only have one chance."

Jeremiah let out a defeated sigh nodded to Peter, understanding what they had to do. He bent his leg behind him, reaching for his ankle and keeping it out of Craig's line of sight.

Agent Craig couldn't believe what he was reading. Now he knew why his superiors wanted this to stay a secret. If the public knew about all of this, there would be a mass panic. Not everyone would believe it, but those who did... there would be total anarchy in the streets. No one would be safe. The civilized world would tear itself apart.

Jeremiah successfully removed the shrapnel bomb from his ankle. He looked to Peter to make sure that he had the remote ready to use. Peter nodded at him, letting him know he was ready. Jeremiah took care to make sure the top of the bomb remained right side up.

"Alright, I've seen enough," Craig started as Jeremiah slid the bomb over to Craig, ending up right next to his right foot, "It's time to-"

Craig wasn't able to finish his sentence as Peter used the remote in his pocket to make the shrapnel bomb go off. It was accompanied by smoke, so they couldn't see how much damage it had done to Craig. Jeremiah wasted no time in untying Peter so they could make their escape. Peter stood up and helped Jeremiah to his feet.

"I need your help to get out of here," Jeremiah said as he grimaced in pain from putting weight on his wounded leg.

"No problem. Let's go, I don't know if that actually hit him hard enough to kill him," Peter replied.

Limping and using Peter as support, the two men left the cabin as quickly as they could. They made their way to the car that they had parked just a quarter of a mile away from the cabin. They had wanted to make the cabin look uninhabited by keeping the car parked further away. Jeremiah was regretting that decision, as every step he took was accompanied by a sharp, shooting pain in his leg.

After a few minutes of hobbling, they finally made it to the car. Peter fumbled in his pocket to grab the keys, but once they had stopped, he was assaulted by another coughing fit. The excitement of that encounter was probably too much for his lungs at this stage.

"Peter, are you okay?" Jeremiah asked.

Peter couldn't answer, so he just handed the keys over to Jeremiah and he recognized this as a sign of trust. He was no longer wearing a bomb, and Peter knew he didn't have to help anymore. Regardless, they had to get away from here. Jeremiah unlocked the driver side door and got in as Peter made his way to the other side of the car. Jeremiah unlocked the passenger door to let Peter in and started the car. Soon, they were on their way through the forest. Jeremiah had no idea where they were supposed to go now, or what they were supposed to do. They had left all the evidence they found at the cabin. All they had was their testimony.

Through his coughing, Peter had a disappointed look on his face that Jeremiah knew was also on his. They now knew the truth, but they were probably the only ones who ever would. Or would ever believe it, at least.

***

Agent Craig laid on the ground. He wasn't really sure what had just happened, he didn't have the mental capacity to process the events at the moment. He couldn't feel the right side of his body. When he tried to open his eyes, he could only open one of them, and all he could see was smoke above his body.

Agent Craig was dying, and he knew it. He could feel the life leaving his body. Those two had gotten away from him with information that could tear the world apart if it ever got out. He tilted his head to the left, where the desk with the computer was. He could see that the computer had gotten destroyed by whatever they had hit him with. He felt relieved. No one would believe two men claiming the world is ending without some kind of evidence. It seems they destroyed all of it in their attempt to escape.

Agent Craig let out a deep breath. He was surprised he could still do as much. He was honestly afraid to look to his right. He feared he'd find a mutilated version of himself. Against his better judgment, he moved his head and found that his right leg was completely gone, his right arm shredded, the bones plainly visible. It must have been some kind of bomb.

For the first time in a very long time, Agent Craig felt afraid. He knew he would die here, and he'd just be another casualty for the United States Government. He had understood that fact since the day he signed on to be their attack dog. But the reality of the situation was much different than what he had reconciled a long time ago.

It was getting harder to breathe every second he lay there. His mind drifted and he thought of Rodney. He had promised Rodney that they would talk. He thought he'd be able to make up for leaving him three years ago. He was so sure that he'd have time to make amends with the man he truly loved. Rodney had even asked if Craig was lying to him again. He had hoped so much that he wasn't, but it looked like he was about to break Rodney's heart again, this time for the last time.

I'm so sorry, Rodney. I tried. I really tried. I love you, Craig thought to himself.

Craig's eye closed and he let out a final labored breath before succumbing to his wounds.

***

They hadn't been driving long when Jeremiah's adrenaline rush started to die down and he felt the effects of the blood loss. He pulled over to the side of the road and waited for Peter's lungs to calm down so he could take the wheel and Jeremiah could rest. After twenty minutes, Peter was ready to continue. They pulled back onto the road and took a highway out of California.

"Where are we going?" Jeremiah asked.

"As far away from the Pacific Ocean as we can possibly get," Peter responded.

"From what I can tell, I don't think it matters how far away we get. The information we lost said something gripped the submarine and crushed it. How do you even run from something that can do that?"

"Well, we have to do something."

"Yeah, we have to tell people. We have to warn everyone!" Jeremiah exclaimed.

"Who's going to believe us?" Peter snapped, "Without the proof in that computer, no one has any reason to take our word."

"You have a reputation for exposing secrets. You've been doing it for years. Why wouldn't the people believe you?"

"Because it isn't like I'm exposing government backed tax fraud here, we're talking about... mythological creatures. This isn't something people just accept! Distrust in the government is one thing, but belief in fucking sea monsters? That's something else entirely."

It was quiet for a few minutes as both men pondered the events and the information they had learned.

"The only thing leaking all of this will accomplish is paint an even bigger target on our backs," Peter said finally.

Jeremiah sat in silence for the next few miles. They were still a few hours from leaving California. Running away can't be the only play they have left. There had to be something they can do.

"Hey Peter," Jeremiah started, "You read more of those files than I did. Was there anything else on these 'Children of the Sea?'"

"Not really. Only that the Feds found the bodies the transmission told them about. They tried to find these 'Children of the Sea' people, but all of their manpower got diverted to keeping the lid on everything. Which I can only guess meant killing anyone who got too close to finding the truth."

"Maybe we can find them," Jeremiah said.

Peter looked over at him, "Do you have any clues?"

"Well, you're kind of an investigator, aren't you?"

"Something like that."

"Then I don't see why we wouldn't be able to find something. Let's go somewhere at least remotely safe and do our due diligence. Maybe you can find something through some old contacts."

"Actually," Peter said after a few minutes of thinking, "I might know someone."

Peter took the next off ramp he saw, and got back on the highway, heading back into the heart of California.

Chapter 7

Peter and Jeremiah pulled up to a gas station outside of San Diego. Their tank was near empty, and they were almost to their destination. On the off-chance that they'd have to make another getaway, which is something Jeremiah never thought would be an expectation, they didn't want to be caught with their pants down, as it were.

Jeremiah decided to stay in the car, as his leg was still in a lot of pain. He had torn the blanket from the cabin into strips and used it as a makeshift bandage over his wound. He was glad Craig had been such a good shot and missed all of his bones. He'd be limping for a while, but at least he was mobile in some capacity.

Peter pulled his wallet out, revealing many $100 bills. Jeremiah raised one eyebrow at the sight. Peter simply shrugged.

"Having dirt on rich people has its perks," He said frankly.

"I guess it does."

Peter got out of the car to pay for gas while Jeremiah waited. Jeremiah stared out his window, and his mind began to wander. He thought of his wife, and how terrified she must have been at the bottom of the ocean. *I finally know the truth, Sasha. I finally know what happened,* Jeremiah thought, hoping that somehow his wife could hear him.

After a few minutes, Peter got back into the car, "Alright, we're good to go. We should be there in about half an hour."

"Who exactly are we going to go see?" Jeremiah asked.

Peter started the car and drove off before answering, "Her name is Jana Simmons. She, uh... she works at Sea World."

"We're getting information from a Sea World employee?" Jeremiah asked, bewildered.

"Yeah, but she's seen some strange things lately. She's been trying to get in contact with me, but I was ignoring her in favor of, you know, what we already did. But now that we know what happened down there, some of what she's been saying sounds more suspicious than ever," Peter said.

"Suspicious how?"

"Suspicious like creepy looking people showing up and everything in the tanks acting strangely."

"How do we know she isn't just trying to lure you there to get the cash reward for turning you in to the authorities?"

"Well," Peter began, "We don't. But we really don't have anything else to go off of at this point. We're going to have to trust her."

"That is... extremely out of character for you," Jeremiah replied.

"Giant sea monsters are extremely out of character for the world that I'm used to. I guess there's changes happening all around us."

"Aren't you supposed to be off the grid? How can someone be trying to get in contact with you when the government can't even find you?"

"Well, no one can really get in contact with me. There are avenues through which someone can *try* to talk to me. Of course, they'll fail, but I'll know that they tried. If it's something that sounds like I should take a look at it, *I* contact *them*," Peter explained.

"How do you even do something like that without getting caught? Or at the very least getting traced and pursued?"

"Untraceable IPs. Mirrors in foreign countries. Complicated internet shit. I've made sure that my online presence can't be tracked through various means. I've made our government's intelligence department's lives very difficult that way."

"Internet and computer talk give me a headache. I'm an old-fashioned typewriter kind of guy."

"Rest your head until we get to where we're going then. I have a feeling the headaches are just beginning for us."

***

"I thought we were going to Sea World," Jeremiah said.

"No, I said she works at Sea World. It's 3:00AM, why would she be at work?" Peter responded, as they pulled up to a house in the suburbs of San Diego. It looked quaint enough. It was a one-story beige colored house with a green painted roof and a single car garage.

"To your point, it is 3:00AM, what makes you think she'll even answer?" Jeremiah asked.

"Because, from her messages and voicemails, she's quite paranoid. You ever hear of people who suffer from paranoia keeping a regular sleeping schedule?"

"I guess not," Jeremiah answered as they got out of the car.

It was cold for a Fall night, but that shouldn't be too surprising given the erratic weather recently. It must be below 40 degrees Fahrenheit, when it should be around 70. These events were playing havoc with the climate.

Jeremiah hobbled up to the door, thankfully there weren't any steps to climb to get there. Peter didn't wait for him to catch up before ringing the doorbell. Not too long after ringing the bell, a worried looking woman answered. She was short, probably 5'2", with blonde hair. Physically fit, she was probably a dolphin trainer at Sea World, given her physique. She wore a baggy jacket and sweat pants, her hair pulled into a messy bun.

"Mr. Jacobson?" she asked, almost instantly recognizing Peter.

"Yes, Miss Simmons. I'm here to talk about the strange people you've seen," Peter replied.

"Please, call me Jana. Who's he?" She asked, scrutinizing Jeremiah.

"This is my associate, David. Don't worry about him," Peter said. Jeremiah was a bit taken aback at Peter's lie. He'd be sure to ask about that later.

Jana looked at him suspiciously for a moment before speaking, "Alright, come on in. You're going to want to hear what I have to say."

The two men walked inside the house. Jeremiah noticed Jana looking around outside before closing the door and locking it with a deadbolt. Peter wasn't kidding about her paranoia. Quickly, Jana directed them to her living room, if you could call it that. She had no real furniture, only a couple of chairs with TV dinner trays in front of them. Peter, Jeremiah and Jana all sat down. Jeremiah looked around the room. There were endless amounts of books piled into every corner, some of them serving as a makeshift stand for her TV, which looked rather old. He couldn't see into the kitchen or any other room, the only lights on were in the living room where they sat.

"Alright, so, start at the beginning," Peter said calmly.

Jana seemed to remember something and went over to one of the piles of books next to her, looking at the covers until she found the one she was looking for. She opened it up without sitting back down and began reading. Peter and Jeremiah exchanged a look, Jeremiah's expression clearly saying that this woman seemed a bit out of her gourd.

"Alright, here it is. I've been keeping journals all my life, and this is the one that has the beginning of their appearances. About 14 or 15 months ago, I started getting this weird feeling that I was being watched and followed. I tried not to think about it and told myself I was being more paranoid than usual, but then about a month ago, these creepy pale people started showing up. First just in random places like the grocery store, then around my work. I remember thinking they were odd because it was the middle of summer and they were wearing black hoodies," Jana said.

"But that wasn't the only weird thing. Any time they went near any tanks with any animals in them, all the animals would immediately start moving towards them, but not in a violent way. Like they were trying to get to these people through the glass. It happened every time any of them showed up, without fail. I tried bringing it up to my boss whenever it happened, but they told me not to harass the customers.

"So, I tried to let it go. But they kept coming back. It was something like once a week that one of these freaks would come to Sea World, just to go near certain animals, rile them up, and then leave. I didn't want to confront any of them, because the one time I actually did get a good look..." Jana said.

"What is it?" Peter asked.

"Well... One of them was standing near the employee entrance to my work, and I saw his face. It looked like... It looked pruned. As if he'd been in the water for too long, like what happens to your hands in a pool or a bathtub. It surprised me, and I couldn't get any words out before he walked away."

Peter and Jeremiah exchanged a look before Peter spoke, "When was the last time one of them was there? At your work?"

Jana thought for a moment, then looked down at her journal to confirm her thoughts, "About two days ago, last time I worked. I think it was someone different, they didn't acknowledge me at all. I wasn't too far, so I know they didn't seem to care I was there."

"So, do you keep logs of when they show up, what times, for how long, information like that?" Jeremiah asked.

Jana shot him a suspicious look and narrowed her eyes at him. It was clear that she didn't trust Jeremiah in the slightest. Well, she didn't trust 'David,' as she thought he was called.

"Jana," Peter said calmly, "He's a friend, you can trust him."

Jana kept her gaze focused on Jeremiah for a few more seconds before she visibly relaxed and let out a deep sigh, "Yes. I make sure I have meticulous records of everything that happens in my life."

"Everything?" Peter asked, "So, you don't keep regular journals, you keep data logs?"

"That's right. It, uh... it helps with my anxiety. And, apparently, it's going to pay off for you and your..." Jana stopped to look at Jeremiah, "...Friend."

Jana looked down at the journal in her hands and started flipping to the end of it. She followed lines with her index finger, mouthing the words as she read.

"Alright, so, the last time was Saturday afternoon. 2:18PM, to be exact. At least that's when I spotted him. Or her, I couldn't really tell under the baggy clothes they wear. And I didn't see their face this time around. They were there until 3:05PM, and during that time, they stayed near the tanks with our exotic fish. From what I saw, in between actually having to work, this person walked around this exhibit, placed their hands-on various tanks, the fish swam to them, and then they would walk away," Jana explained.

"Is there any sort of pattern to when they visit? Any kind of schedule they keep?" Peter asked.

Jana shook her head, "I tried looking for something like that. But it's always completely random. Sometimes they'll show up Monday morning and stay for five minutes, other times they'll show up on a Thursday, near closing time. But they do always show up at least once a week. My days off change every week, so it's possible they've shown up more than once. But I always seem to catch them there once a week."

"That's a bit strange," Jeremiah said.

"What is?" Peter asked.

"That they always show up when Jana is working. That's peculiar. None of them have ever approached you or tried to talk to you directly?" Jeremiah asked.

"No, never. The only interaction I've had with any of them was the one I saw face-to-face in front of my work," Jana answered.

"Do you think they want her to see them?" Jeremiah asked Peter.

"I don't see why they would. I guess we'll find out about that as well. When's your next day of work?" Peter asked.

"Tomorrow," Jana answered, "Well, technically it's today."

"We have to go with her," Jeremiah said to Peter.

"No, *you* have to go with her. I'm not exactly a subtle figure in the crowd these days. My face has been plastered all over the news. If anyone there makes me, it's over. No one knows you're with me, or what you look like, for that matter."

Jeremiah thought about it for a second before responding, "Alright. You make a good point. Jana, I'll go with you tomorrow," he looked over at Peter, "Do you still have those communicators from earlier?"

"Yeah, they're in the car."

"Good. Any chance you have a third one?" Jeremiah asked.

"No, unfortunately. Just the two. I didn't foresee needing to have a third one," Peter replied.

"I feel like there are a lot of things happening lately that you did not foresee. Alright. Peter, you and I will wear one, and I'll just do my best to stick close to Jana, so she can signal me when she sees one of them. Once that happens, I'll let you know, and I'll tail them through the park until they leave. After that, I'll follow them until they get... wherever it is they go afterwards. Then we can meet back up here and plan our next step."

"Why not just go in right then?" Jana asked.

Jeremiah motioned to the wound in his thigh, "I don't know if you noticed, but I'm not exactly in the best physical condition at the moment. And we don't know if these people are dangerous or not. It's better to plan what we're going to do first."

Jana closed her eyes and thought for a moment, "Wait. Alright, I'm glad you guys are here, and I'm glad you want to help out. But what happened to you? And, and I can't believe I haven't asked this yet, what's in it for you?"

Peter sighed, "What happened to him has to do with these people, we think. And, if they are who we think they are, then they have answers to some questions that we have. It's in our best interest to help you."

"So, who do you think these people are?" Jana asked.

Jeremiah looked to Peter to answer her question. Jeremiah wasn't sure exactly how much information was safe to divulge to her at this point. It was still possible that the people she's been seeing have nothing to do with the Children of the Sea. Peter looked back at Jeremiah and nodded.

"We're using you as bait here, so it only makes sense that we tell you what it's for. We're looking for a group of people that call themselves 'The Children of the Sea.' They're, uh... they're the reason why tides have been strange and the weather has been erratic, basically. And we're trying to figure out how they're doing it. And how to make them stop. That's the gist of it," Peter said.

"Why do you think this is them?" Jana asked.

"It's the only lead we've got," Peter replied, "So, it's either looking into this or being completely lost."

Jana nodded, "Alright. In that case, we should all get some rest. I have to be there by 10:30AM to help get ready for opening. You two can sleep in this living room. I don't really have extra blankets or pillows or anything..."

"Don't worry. We'll be fine here," Jeremiah said quickly.

Jana nodded, stood up and walked out of the room. Jeremiah couldn't see out of the living room but heard her footsteps as she walked across the house to where her bedroom was.

Jeremiah stood from the chair and groaned as his thigh protested the movement, "I think I finally understand people who are against guns," he said as he lightly touched around his wound.

Peter chuckled and coughed despite himself as he got out of his chair and sat on the floor, presumably where he was going to sleep. Jeremiah decided to do the same and lightly lowered himself down onto the floor. He kept his injured leg stretched out in front of him. When Jeremiah looked back over at Peter, he was already laying down, facing away from him.

Jeremiah thought of the likelihood of their group actually being able to make some sort of difference, given the various handicaps they had all been dealt. Peter's cancer, Jeremiah's leg wound, and Jana's seemingly crippling anxiety. It would be an interesting ride, indeed, seeing how all of this will play out in the following days.

And then his mind wandered back to the entirety of the day's events. The suspicions and revelations that had basically assaulted his psyche. Added to the physical damage he sustained, he wasn't sure how he was still going. *I helped kill someone today,* Jeremiah thought to himself. A man was dead because of his and Peter's actions. He probably had a life outside of whatever his job was. People who cared about him, people who would wonder what happened to him, just as Jeremiah had wondered what happened to Sasha. He had inflicted the pain that he had suffered so long on an entirely new group of people. The pain of not knowing what happened to someone they love.

Jeremiah didn't sleep that night.

Chapter 8

Jeremiah squinted through the sunglasses he was wearing up at the sun, high in the sky. It was about noon, now, and still there was no sign of one of these people that Jana had told them about. It was also infuriatingly hot, given how cold the night had been previously. He felt a small tinge of pity for people who had broken bones in their lives. An old friend of his had previously told him that sudden temperature changes were accompanied by acute pain in the areas they had injured.

Jeremiah stood outside of the exhibit that Jana was working in, keeping watch on any passerby's, hoping maybe he would get a glimpse of something. So far, nothing out of the ordinary like Jana had described. Everything seemed to be business-as-usual for Sea World.

"Anything?" Jeremiah heard Peter ask in his ear.

"Nothing yet."

"I don't know why I expected some kind of instant gratification out of this little stake-out of ours."

"Maybe because so much happened in just one day prior to this."

Peter made a noise of agreement and went back to being silent. Jeremiah figured he may as well walk back inside of the exhibit and see if Jana had seen anything. Seeing as she was on the clock, and they were trying to be incognito, they had come up with a way to let each other know if they saw anything out of the ordinary. Jana would look at Jeremiah with wide eyes if she saw something, and Jeremiah would lower his sunglasses at her if he did.

Jeremiah calmly walked back inside and took a quick look around. He'd never been to Sea World before, which meant that many of these fish were alien to him. His wife would either be having a field day or would be appalled at this many fish in captivity. Possibly both. He couldn't help but wonder what her reaction to everything they just discovered would have been. How she would feel about these so-called Children of the Sea. For a moment, he felt like all she would feel was a scientific curiosity. It was how she was. She longed to know more, especially if it involved the ocean.

Jeremiah could see nothing out of the ordinary in his proximity. He looked to Jana, who had probably noticed him as soon as he had entered, and she gave him a simple glance, not indicative of anything. Jeremiah sighed, just as disappointed as Peter was at the lack of events. As strange as it seemed, given the severity of the circumstances, Jeremiah had felt tinges of excitement at what they were doing. It felt as if they were trying to save the world here. Though, he knew intellectually, that all they're doing is trying to gather more information. He wasn't sure if Peter even knew what they would do with said information, other than go public with it. He wasn't sure if it would even make a difference.

Jeremiah walked around the exhibit, a glimmer of hope still in him that they would find a substantial lead today. He stepped wrong and his wounded leg protested in the form of a sharp pain shooting up his thigh. Jeremiah grimaced and gripped around the wound instinctively. He was going to join some kind of anti-gun rally when this was all over, with the bullet hole in his thigh as his justification. Assuming there would be such a thing when this was all over. He didn't know what the world had in store in the coming years.

"How about now?" Peter asked in the earpiece.

"I will let you know. Asking every five minutes only disappoints me when I have to tell you that nothing is happening."

"Fine. I just don't like feeling so... so *bored.*"

Jeremiah concurred. But he kept walking around, occasionally glancing at Jana to see if she had spotted anything.

For the rest of the day, they saw many different types of people walking through the exhibit. People with families, couples, kids running around and ignoring their parents, some people on their own with a fascination of undersea life, students, you name it. But nothing out of the ordinary, and nothing that helped them.

***

"You know, I imagined stake-outs to be more exciting than that," Jeremiah said, as they drove back to Jana's house. Peter drove as Jeremiah stared out the window. The night was as hot and humid as the day had been.

"They're almost always like this. It's a lot like fishing."

"That's the simile you want to go with? Really? All things considered, that's kind of in bad taste."

"It's the best I could think of," Peter replied frankly.

"If they're always like that, why were you so bored and anxious?" Jeremiah asked.

"We're not exactly in a normal situation here. The stakes are much higher than they've ever been. I suppose it's having an effect on-" Peter was interrupted by a coughing fit.

Jeremiah quickly grabbed a hold of the wheel and steered them to the side of the road. Peter applied the brakes without Jeremiah having to say anything. Peter's coughing fits were becoming more frequent and more violent.

"Jesus, Peter."

"I'm okay," Peter replied after a few more moments of coughing.

"No, you're not. When is the last time you saw a doctor?"

"You know a lot of doctors who wouldn't turn me in to the authorities? If so, please, I'd love a referral. If not, I'm just going to have to deal with this until..."

"Until what?" Jeremiah asked.

"Until I either die or everyone else does."

Jeremiah didn't respond to that.

"What's my cancer in comparison to the lives of everyone who could die if they don't have fair warning? You were right, Jeremiah. When you said that we have to do something."

"Removed from the adrenaline of the moment, I have to ask. What are we going to do when... *if* we find them?" Jeremiah asked.

"My hope is that we'll be able to figure out a way to stop what's coming."

"And if we can't?"

"Then we go public. Tell everyone who will listen. Get people out of here, away from the Pacific Ocean."

"You said that that would only paint a target on our backs," Jeremiah said.

"If we reach that point, there will be a target on everyone's backs. We won't have any other choice. Right now, we have a small lead, a small thread we can follow. So that's what we're doing. Until we run out of options."

Peter and Jeremiah pulled up to Jana's house. They had stayed behind for about an hour after Jana was off work, Jeremiah still looking around and Peter waiting, just in case. It was about 8:00PM now, and there was only a faint light coming from Jana's living room window. Jeremiah assumed she must be writing the day's events into one of her journals.

Peter parked, and they both got out. Jeremiah limping weakly to the front door. Standing and walking all day on his injured leg had not done him any favors, and he was looking forward to laying down, even if it was on that hard floor with no real comforts. Peter walked ahead of him. Jana had given him a key to her house before they had left for their stake-out, so they could come and go from their makeshift base of operations as was necessary. Peter reached into his pocket to grab the key when the front door swung open, revealing a distressed looking Jana. She had one hand behind her back.

"You two need to get inside. Right now," she said adamantly.

Without a word, the two men walked into the house, past Jana, who would not take her eyes off of them or turn her back to them. Jeremiah wondered what was happening. He knew she was paranoid, but what had set this off?

As soon as they were all inside the house, Jana locked her door, and pulled a gun from behind her back, pointing it in their direction. A mixture of fear and conviction was visible on her face.

"Jana... what are you doing?" Peter asked.

"You... you killed a cop!" Jana exclaimed at Peter.

"What?" both men asked in unison.

"You killed the cop? You just told me not to worry about him!" Jeremiah exclaimed.

"I didn't kill him! I left him tied up!"

"Liar!" Jana shouted, "I just saw on the news. It said that a cop who was investigating a tip on your location was found tied up with a bullet hole in his head."

"I swear, I didn't-" Peter was interrupted by Jana just then.

"And you!" She yelled, pointing her gun towards Jeremiah, "Your name isn't David. Your name is Jeremiah Wilkins."

"Wait, what?" Jeremiah asked.

"Don't play stupid. It said on the news that you're a suspected accomplice. There was a picture of you and everything."

Great. Now I'm wanted by the police, too. Life keeps getting better.

"Now, you two are going to tell me everything, and I mean *everything*, or I am going to call the cops and hold you here at gunpoint until they get here."

"Okay, okay. Just, lower the gun, and we can talk about everything," Peter said calmly.

"No way. You're a murderer. Why would I do what you say?"

"Because I didn't kill that police officer. I swear it, I left him tied up and we drove away. I'm not a killer. Neither is he. He's a teacher for Christ's sake."

"Professor," Jeremiah corrected.

"Do you *really* think now is the right time to correct someone?" Peter asked, incredulously.

Jana looked at them suspiciously for a full minute, before motioning with her gun for them to go into her living room. They walked ahead of her and each took a seat next to each other, facing her. She did not sit, she stood with her gun still raised.

"Jana, please sit. What we're going to tell you... it's going to be hard to swallow," Peter said.

"Fine. But I'm not lowering the gun," Jana said as she sat down across from them, gun still raised.

"Alright. It started over eleven years ago..." Peter began.

***

"Looks like the girl made some friends."

She smiled, "Some very clumsy friends, it would seem. It was entirely too easy to spy on them."

"Is it time?"

"Perhaps. She's got those two looking for us. Maybe we should let them find us. Who knows, maybe they could be of use to us as well," she answered.

"With all due respect, madam, why do we even want her to join us? She's a paranoid and anxiety riddled mess."

"Because, she is a child of the sea, just as we are. And we don't leave our brothers and sisters on their own. She is the way she is because we've taken so long to find her. The rest of us have been a part of this family since we were children. Here she is, a grown woman, with no clue as to her real identity."

"But... will she acclimate properly? Will she even *want* to join us?"

"I believe so. And if I'm wrong, we've dealt with this kind of thing before. Besides, it doesn't matter too much at this point. If she wants to live, she'll join us," she answered.

"What about her friends? The whistleblower and his companion?"

"They want answers, don't they? Why don't we give them some?"

"Madam, is that wise?"

Her smile faded, "Keep questioning me, little brother. You'll quickly find out how far that'll take you."

He visibly panicked at her warning, "I apologize! Please forgive me!"

"Oh, don't worry. You haven't angered me nearly enough for... retribution."

His skin went cold at her use of that word. Everyone here knew what that meant. Everyone here feared what that meant.

"Since you're so curious about my motives, why don't you be the one to reveal yourself to them?"

"...Y-yes, madam. When would you like me to do so?" he stammered, nervously.

"Tomorrow. We wouldn't want our new sister and her friends to get desperate, would we? That would just be rude," she said, her smile returning.

"Yes. As you wish. Will that be all, madam?"

"Yes. Leave me, now," she commanded.

"Thank you, Madam Salem," he said cordially, before leaving her presence.

Madam Salem listened to his echoing footsteps as he quickly walked away. How she loved the fear in the hearts of her underlings. It brought her immense pleasure. The sound of his footsteps was quickly taken over by the sound of dripping water, spreading through the cave she resided in. Musty, would be the best word to describe her immediate environment. She didn't mind. In fact, she loved it.

She walked across her platform to the small alcove that led to her bed chambers. She remembered how long it had taken her underlings to sculpt her platform and her bedchambers. They did whatever she asked of them, regardless of how difficult the task was. So many hands had been ruined doing this particular one. She reveled in it.

She sat at her bed, the foundation made of stone with a soft, if not a little moldy, mattress on top. Sitting there, she shut her eyes to feel *them*.

They were so close.

It was almost time.

She smiled.

***

An hour later, Jana set the gun down on a stack of journals beside her. She had stopped aiming it at the two men a while ago but was just now okay with the idea of not holding it anymore. Jeremiah let out a sigh of relief, happy to no longer be under the threat of being shot. Again.

"Okay, then," Jana said.

After a moment of silence, Jeremiah spoke, "That's it?"

"Yeah. That's it."

"I expected more of a reaction, to be honest. I could hardly believe it when we found out," Jeremiah said.

"No, it... it makes sense," Jana replied.

"It does? I'm *still* trying to wrap my head around what we learned and what we're trying to do, but you think it makes sense?" Jeremiah asked, incredulously.

"I guess it's my turn to explain."

Peter and Jeremiah exchanged a confused look before Jana began to speak again.

"This is going to sound crazy. Or, it would, under different circumstances. But... I've always kind of felt something. Like something trying to lead me to the ocean. It's like... this is difficult to explain, but it's felt like something from deep down was calling to me, asking me for help, or something. There are times when it's nearly impossible to resist, and I've always felt crazy because of it. I think it might be what's caused my... well..." Jana motioned towards all the journals around her, to illustrate her point.

"Alright, I know we're pretty deep in this shit now, but this keeps getting weirder," Jeremiah said, "By which, I mean, it's getting really hard to pretend what we're doing isn't inherently insane. Sea monsters, a cult, and now someone who can feel something from the ocean calling to her? Are we in way over our heads here?"

"No doubt about that. But like you said, we're pretty deep in it now," Peter replied before turning his attention back to Jana, "Will you keep helping us, then? Maybe you can learn more about... why you feel this calling from the ocean."

Jana hesitantly looked between the both of them before nodding her head and speaking, "Yes. I'll keep helping. But we have to be way more careful from now on. Both of your faces were on the news tonight, if anyone recognizes either of you, this whole thing is over."

"She's right," Peter said, "Before tonight, you were completely anonymous. Now, you're almost as popular as I am. It's going to be much harder to operate out in the open."

"Why don't I just keep wearing some sunglasses and maybe a hoodie?" Jeremiah asked.

"Because this isn't a movie, and things like that don't *actually* work," Peter replied.

"The people we're looking for literally walk around in hoodies and no one pays attention to them!" Jeremiah exclaimed.

"Their faces probably weren't all over the evening news. We have to figure something else out."

Jana cleared her throat to get their attention, "I could wear the earpiece. I mean, I'm in there anyway. You two can hide somewhere and wait for my signal. That way, neither of you are out in the open, and when you follow them, neither of you will be by yourself. In case they're dangerous, like you said."

Peter thought about it for a moment, "Yeah. Alright, that sounds like it'll work. Hopefully tomorrow is the day one of them shows up. Every day we have to do this, we risk getting caught. That's the worst-case scenario for anyone who knows anything of any importance. No one will listen to us from behind bars."

"That's assuming we'd even get arrested, and not immediately killed to shut us up," Jeremiah said.

"Let's... let's not dwell on that. Let's just get some rest, so we're ready for tomorrow. Jana, is your shift tomorrow the same as today's?"

"Yeah, same shift on any day that I work."

"Alright, so it'll be almost the same drill as today," Peter said.

Jana nodded before she stood without a word and walked, presumably, to her bedroom. It was still early, and Jeremiah was sure that none of them were particularly ready to go to sleep, but it was probably for the best to rest themselves, if even just mentally. *It just keeps getting better and better, doesn't it?* Jeremiah thought to himself.

Chapter 9

The next morning, they were all getting ready to leave. Jeremiah and Jana had both been up early while Peter kept sleeping, letting out the occasional cough while he was under. Jeremiah could tell that Peter was getting worse. The excitement combined with his neglecting of his cancer was beginning to weigh on him more heavily than anticipated. Jeremiah knew it was only a matter of time before he couldn't keep up.

Jeremiah had realized that he had a new predicament: he didn't have any clothes with him. He had foolishly thought that going along with Peter would be a quick errand, so he hadn't packed anything before agreeing to accompany him. Peter, being the planner, had two suitcases full of his own clothes sitting in his trunk. Jeremiah had tried to put on some of

Peter's clothes, but he was much taller and broader than the clothes would comfortably allow.

Jana had been kind enough to run to the closest thrift shop and pick him up a few shirts, two pairs of jeans and some underwear. She had also allowed him access to her washer and dryer.

Jeremiah didn't know exactly what he had expected, but when he finally roamed Jana's house to look for the washing room, he was a bit surprised to see that it was actually very well kept. Part of him was disappointed that it wasn't a consistent mess of anxiety driven hoarding throughout, like her living room was, but it made finding his way around a simpler task.

Jana had welcomed them both to use her home as they required, which meant that Jeremiah would finally be able to take a shower and try to clean off the vague scent of bad news and unexpected excitement. He was a bit taken aback at Jana's sudden hospitality, given that she had just been aiming a gun at both of them the night before. It really did pay to be honest with people, he thought.

Jeremiah walked through the hallway until he reached the bathroom, the second door on his left. He had the clothes that Jana had purchased for him in a bag he clutched in his right hand, along with a towel she had given him under his arm. Setting them down next to the sink, he walked to the shower and turned the water on, scrutinizing the three knobs to make sure he was turning on the hot water and not the freezing cold. It was always confusing in houses that he wasn't used to.

Once he was sure he had the water running the way he wanted it to, he stripped off his dirty clothes and let them fall to the floor. He'd collect them afterwards. Now naked, he looked down at his left thigh and the bandage wrapped around it. Peter had had a first aid kit in his car, and he was a surprisingly competent medic, for lack of a better word. He had disinfected the wound and wrapped it, with gauze covering both the entrance and exit wounds from the gunshot.

Jeremiah unwrapped the bandage and lifted the gauze slightly to look at the wound, which he had refused to do up until this point. It didn't look nearly as bad as he had imagined it would. The wounds had already started scabbing over and they looked like they were healing properly, as far as he could tell. This was one of those moments where he wondered if maybe he should have listened to his mother and tried to go to medical school.

The bathroom was now being filled with steam from the hot water, and Jeremiah realized how long he had been scrutinizing his leg wound. Carefully, he stepped into the shower and let the hot water soothe his body and mind, calming him. Hot showers had always been a great source of stress relief for him. Sasha had disliked them, preferring lukewarm water to the scalding heat that Jeremiah was so fond of. Jeremiah couldn't help thoughts of his wife popping into his head at moments like these.

Jeremiah quickly cleaned himself and used some of Jana's shampoo to wash his hair. When he was done, he turned the water off and toweled himself dry as fast as he could. The hot water had made the temperature seem comparably much colder than before he had gotten in.

He opened the bag of clothes and picked some from the very simple wardrobe that had been procured for him. A simple black T-Shirt and jeans, with blue boxer briefs underneath. When he lifted the clothes out of the bag, he noticed that Jana had also purchased deodorant, a toothbrush, and toothpaste for him. He made a mental note to thank her for her consideration.

He dressed quickly, spent a few minutes brushing his teeth and used his fingers to comb his hair as best as he could. When he was ready, he exited the bathroom with his dirty clothes under his arm, along with the towel, and the rest of his new clothes still in the bag with his deodorant and toothbrush. The toothpaste was left in the bathroom, next to the sink. He left the door to the bathroom ajar, allowing the room to air the steam out.

When he got back to the living room, he found Peter, already dressed and seemingly ready, with no sign of Jana.

"Where's Jana?" Jeremiah asked.

"I don't know, she wasn't around when I woke up. Probably a good thing, since I had to change, and you were in the bathroom for so long."

"Sorry about that. I missed showering."

"It's been two days, man."

"I don't really like going even one day without a shower," Jeremiah stated, matter-of-factly.

"You get used to it, trust me."

Before Jeremiah could answer, the front door swung open and Jana walked in. Her face was pale, and she looked terrified. She turned to the living room to face Jeremiah and Peter, and she opened her mouth to try to speak, but no words came out.

Jeremiah's expression grew concerned, "Jana, what's wrong?"

Jana's mouth opened again, but still she did not speak. She merely used her hand to motion towards something behind her.

"Jana?" Peter asked, moving to stand beside Jeremiah, worry painted on his face.

"Good evening, gentlemen," said a masculine voice.

From behind Jana, a man wearing black blazer, dark blue T-Shirt and black slacks stepped forward. The man was tall and slender, the blazer didn't quite fit him, but gave his presence more of an imposing sense than he would have without it. He had tanned brown skin, and could possibly be Latino, but there were no hints in the man's accent when he spoke. He had a deadly serious expression on his face, but his pose as he stood next to Jana felt more relaxed. That combination gave Jeremiah an eerie feeling about their uninvited guest.

"Jana, why don't you go stand next to your friends, hmm?" the man said to Jana.

Without a word, Jana complied with the man and quickly walked forward, taking her place next to Peter and facing the man in front of them. He flashed a grin, but it wasn't comforting in the least. A grin on this man's face felt like more cause to be worried than anything else. Jeremiah felt a pit forming in his stomach.

The man then casually closed the door he stood next to and locked it. Every move he made frightened Jeremiah even more. He looked over to Peter, who he felt would be holding it together better than he was. By the look on his face, he was more concerned than afraid. Jana, however, looked terrified.

"I'm going to make this very simple," the man began, "You're all going to come with me, and you will be glad that you did... especially you," he said as he pointed a finger at Jana.

"The last person who told us we were going to go somewhere with him met with some less than pleasant consequences," Peter said.

Jeremiah raised his eyebrows at Peter and his bluff. They had had a bomb the last time they were in this position. This time, they had nothing to defend themselves with. Jeremiah wasn't sure, but he felt that they wouldn't stand a chance in a fight against anyone in their current condition.

"You know, I was told to bring all three of you back with me, but I don't know that She would mind if I was forced to kill most of you. As long as *she* comes back with me, I think I'll still be in the clear."

Jeremiah felt confusion at that last bit, "Wait, you only need Jana?"

"Need is the operative word in that statement, yes. You two are, in my opinion, wholly unnecessary."

Jeremiah looked at Peter, who now looked as confused as he felt.

"So, you're not here to arrest us?" Peter asked.

"If it's all the same to you, could we have this conversation in the car? She doesn't like to be kept waiting," the man said.

"Who?" Jeremiah asked.

The man rubbed his temple in frustration. The frightening demeanor was now all but gone, and he seemed to just want to get on with it, "Christ on the cross, would you just get in the fucking car? Trust me, we're going somewhere that you all wanted to go anyway."

Jeremiah felt like they didn't really have a choice. He began to step forward to accompany the man, which was probably just another in his recent long line of ill-advised decisions, when Jana threw her arm out and stopped him.

"Wait! His face! He's one of *them!*" Jana shouted.

Jeremiah and Peter both looked at the man before them, who was now grinning that unsettling grin again, with a hint of frustration in his brow. Aside from some laugh lines he had not taken note of, indicating that this man was probably well into his 40s, Jeremiah didn't notice anything overtly strange. He definitely didn't look the way Jana had described the people she had seen at work.

"Jana, he looks normal," Peter said, disappointment in his voice.

"No! No way! His face, he looks just like what I said! His skin looks like it's been in the water for too long! Pruned!" Jana was hysterical.

"This is all extremely amusing, really, but as I've said, She doesn't like to be kept waiting. It won't just be my ass if she grows impatient, so let's get a move on. I'll answer some of your questions on the way, as per her Her instructions."

Peter gently grabbed Jana by her shoulders to try to calm her down, "Jana, let's do what he says. We'll finally get some answers. Isn't that what you want?" Peter asked softly.

Jana took two deep breaths before finally nodding her head in approval, never once taking her eyes off of the man.

"Wonderful," the man said, before opening the door and motioning for them to walk through ahead of him, "Right this way."

The trio walked through the door, following the man's instructions. His being behind them somehow made the situation more tense than when he was facing them. When they walked out, they saw that he had a medium sized SUV parked on the sidewalk in front of Jana's house. It was a dark blue Honda Pilot, Jeremiah was unsure of the year, but it looked slightly old. Mud graced the lower part of the vehicle, as if it had just driven through a dirt road after rainfall.

The man directed them towards his vehicle, unlocked it and motioned for Jana to sit in the front passenger seat next to him, leaving Peter and Jeremiah in the back. As soon as the three of them were in and buckled, that's when the man entered the vehicle himself and started the engine. Within minutes, they were on their way. Jeremiah felt uneasy, but he didn't know if he was afraid or anxious. Maybe both.

After a few minutes on the road, Jana finally spoke, "Why can't they see your... your face?"

He chuckled, "I'm fairly certain they can see my face."

"You know what I mean!"

He gave her a sidelong glance before answering, "They're not one of us, Jana. They can't see the truth."

"What does *that* mean?" Peter asked.

He looked at Peter through his rearview mirror, "I'll go ahead and let Her answer that particular question. I wouldn't want to give away too much."

"You said you'd give us answers," Peter said.

"I said I'd give you some answers. Ask questions I can answer, and I will," he said firmly.

Jeremiah tried to keep quiet during this exchange. This man had made it quite clear that he and Peter were disposable, so he didn't want to say anything to make his value to them drop even further. Peter didn't seem to have that fear, his tone obstinate and demanding.

"Fine," Peter began, "What's your name?"

"There's a question I can answer. I was born Andrew Wilson, but I haven't been called that in a really long time. In fact, most of us don't even remember our birth names anymore. I only do because I have to."

"Why do you have to?" Peter asked.

"You ever try venturing out into the world without a name? Without an ID?" Andrew asked.

"So... what, most of you... *people* don't leave?" Peter asked.

"No, most of us don't. Your tone is bothering me," Andrew said.

Peter swallowed at Andrew's statement, which was said in an extremely malicious and threatening tone. Peter was finally starting to feel the fear that Jeremiah had felt earlier. Jeremiah saw Peter visibly shrink back into his seat, as opposed to the position he had held, leaning forward in defiance of this man's frightening presence.

"Okay. I have one more question," Peter said, almost whispering.

"I can't wait."

"Your people... are you the Children of the Sea?" Peter asked, his voice shaking in anticipation of his answer.

Andrew's face didn't change expression when he answered, "Yes."

Peter's face held an expression of both fear and excitement. Jeremiah knew why. They had found the ones they were looking for, but they were also currently their 'guests,' which was his polite way of saying they were their prisoners.

Andrew turned his attention to Jeremiah in the rearview mirror, "You. Don't you have anything to ask? Your silence is making me... uneasy."

Jeremiah thought for a moment, trying to think of a question to ask. He had to play along if he wanted to stay alive long enough to see how everything played out. He wanted to be smart about everything.

Finally, he thought of something, "When are they coming?" he asked.

Jeremiah watched as Andrew's face spread into the most sinister smile he had ever seen in person, rather than on a TV screen. Andrew let out a slight chuckle before answering his question, "Soon."

***

Twenty-five minutes later, Andrew pulled the SUV into a parking lot very close to La Jolla Shores, a beach not too far from where they were staying. The parking lot was situated so that the beach was a short walk directly in front of them, the pier a small uphill walk to the right.

He'd never been here before, and he was only slightly surprised to see how empty the beach looked. There were maybe two people out on their beach towels. He then looked to the pier and saw a couple of groups of people, nothing substantial.

He imagined it would be hard to convince people to go to the beach these days, given the unpredictable nature of these new tides. He had seen on the news over a year ago that when this all began; a few children had been swept into the ocean. Since then, beaches hadn't been too popular.

"Follow me," Andrew commanded.

Jeremiah walked with Peter and Jana, not trailing too far behind Andrew. He was leading them towards the beach, but also towards the pier. It seemed they wouldn't be going up to the pier, but rather to the support beams below it.

Jeremiah was a bit nervous at the direction they were headed in. His wife had tried to teach him, but Jeremiah had never really been a strong swimmer. It wasn't something he liked to admit, and he was foolish for thinking that chasing a group called "The Children of the Sea" wasn't eventually going to require going into some kind of body of water.

"Uh.. Andrew?" Jeremiah called ahead of him. Andrew didn't acknowledge his call, but he continued anyway, "Are we... swimming somewhere?"

Andrew turned his head slightly but kept walking, "No. Not yet, anyway."

Great, Jeremiah thought.

Andrew led them to a support beam closer to the shallow end of the waters, but it was obvious that it wasn't always the shallow end. There were barnacles stuck to the beam that looked like they'd been wet not too long ago.

Andrew stopped walking when they were on the opposite side of the beam, and everyone stopped with him, "Make sure you stand close. Right there," Andrew said as he pointed to the ground around him. Everyone complied.

No one asked him what they were doing, which Jeremiah thought was strange. Maybe they were both trying to be careful with their words as well. Andrew's biting and threatening tone may have changed their minds.

Before long, the ground beneath them began to shift slightly. Jeremiah flinched at the feeling, having no idea what was happening. When he looked down, he saw that the ground they stood on was sinking. It took him a moment to realize that they stood on some kind of elevator. After a few seconds, all of their heads were below the level of ground they had just been walking on. They all looked up and saw that there was a piece of metal replacing the area that had been lowered.

"I find it incredibly hard to believe that no one has seen someone go down one of these yet. The government was looking for your people, and they never caught on to this?" Peter asked.

"Why would the government follow normal looking people who aren't doing anything suspicious?" Andrew asked.

"Your people walk around in conspicuous clothing and rile up fish at Sea World," Peter said.

"Then why was no one worried except for Jana here?"

He had a good point. From the way Jana tells it, it seemed everyone but her all but ignored them and the effect they had on the fish.

"You tell us," Jana said, finally breaking her silence since they got into the car.

"Because the so-called strange fish behavior you claim to have seen? It doesn't look strange at all to normal people. You notice things they can't. And people wearing hoods? That's commonplace. Everyone loves jackets and sweaters, and I've seen teenagers wearing them in scorching temperatures. There's nothing conspicuous about us."

"What do you mean 'normal people?'" Jana asked.

"She'll explain that to you. As for how no one has seen anyone go down this elevator, did you not notice how empty the beach is? Before the tides ran everyone off with the fear of being swept into the ocean by strong currents and tides, we only ever came and went under the cover of night. But thanks to recent events, we've been much freer than we've ever been."

"I still don't buy it," Peter said.

"You don't have to. That doesn't change the reality of things," Andrew replied.

Soon, they reached the bottom. It was dark, but not quite pitch black. Jeremiah couldn't see more than a few feet in front of him, so their environment was hidden from view. He could see the people around him and the floor, which looked like polished stone. He could hear water dripping and the faraway sound of running water, like a river.

"Let's go," Andrew said, before walking forward. They had no choice but to follow him, as they couldn't really see much else.

Each footstep they took was accompanied by a loud echo and reverberation all around him. It was ingenious, hiding somewhere that had these kinds of acoustics. It would be impossible to sneak into this place effectively. Even the breaths they took came with their own echo.

"What is this place?" Jana said. Her voice no longer sounded afraid or anxious. There was a hint of awe in the way she asked that, as if she was transfixed by something, enamored by their surroundings.

"It's a cave. We're currently heading further into the ocean, and deeper below it. This place was carved out long before I was found and brought here. Not many people here know exactly how this was done, as it predates them as well."

"It's... it's beautiful," Jana said.

"You can see in here?" Peter asked her.

"Yeah. You can't?" Jana asked.

"I can barely see you walking next to me."

"Like I said, she notices things normal people can't. Let's hope you don't lose us in the dark, you might never find your way back," Andrew said, half serious.

Andrew made a sharp right turn, momentarily terrifying Jeremiah that he had lost his lead, but instead followed Jana. Soon, he could see Andrew again, as his eyes were beginning to adjust to the darkness.

"Are we going to see... uh, Her?" Jeremiah asked.

"We are."

"Do you know what she wants with us?" Peter asked.

"With you two? Nothing. With her? Even I don't know. But you'll soon find out for yourselves. I just do what She tells me. Save the rest of your inquiries for Her," Andrew answered.

They remained silent for the rest of the walk, concentrating on not losing each other in the dark winding cave. Turn after turn came, and it became increasingly obvious that there would be no hasty escape from this place. Likely, they would just get lost and die of starvation in here if they tried. It seemed they were truly captives.

Finally, Andrew stopped in front of them and moved to stand to the side. He motioned for them to continue forward without him. Jeremiah could see what looked like a carved doorway, leading somewhere else. It was still too dark to see too far ahead.

"Wait, how will we know where to go?" Jeremiah asked.

Andrew looked intently at Jana, "Follow her. She'll know."

Peter looked to Jana for an answer to that cryptic phrase. Jana responded, "I... I do know..."

"How?" Peter asked.

"I don't know. I just know. It feels like I'm being called again. But it's different this time. I can't explain it." Jana began to walk forward and the men had no choice but to follow her.

They walked through the carved doorway, which opened into what he felt was a much bigger room. He couldn't see where the walls were, as opposed to where they just were. His eyes had adjusted enough to see that far, but in here, there was no way he would be able to. They simply followed Jana's lead and hoped that it didn't end badly.

"I can't believe I forgot to ask, but," Jeremiah began, "Do we have any sort of plan here?"

"I don't think so. I think we're just going to have to go with it for a while and hope for the best," Peter answered.

"That doesn't instill a whole lot of confidence."

"No, it doesn't, but there's not much else we can do. Just try not to piss off... whoever it is we're going to see."

"I wasn't planning on it."

If Jana was listening to them, she gave no indication. She seemed to be almost gliding towards a destination known only to her. They kept pace with her, but just barely. Jeremiah's leg was aching and keeping up with Jana's brisk pace was getting more difficult by the minute.

All of a sudden, Jana stopped. The men stopped short behind her, narrowly missing bumping into her. Jeremiah looked forward and saw a wall of polished stone. A portion of it had chemical streaks all across it, distinguishing it from the rest of the polished stone wall.

Jana held her hand up to the wall, and as soon as she touched it, they all heard it start to move. It slid backwards into the rest of the wall before sliding to the left, revealing an opening. Inside, there was a light that stung Jeremiah's eyes. He held his hands up to shield his gaze. Now his eyes would have to readjust to light.

Jana walked forward into the opening. It took Jeremiah a moment to realize she had started moving forward. Peter still hadn't noticed, so Jeremiah grabbed his arm and pulled him forward. As soon as they were through, the wall replaced itself, closing the opening and sealing them in this new chamber.

As Jeremiah's eyes adjusted, he looked around to see what looked like an extravagant temple. It looked like what he imagined places of worship in Ancient Egypt looking like. There were white silk curtains hiding parts of the temple from sight, and in front of them was a big open space with a large platform at the end.

On the large platform stood a woman. Jeremiah couldn't make out many of her features, only that she had pitch black hair and that she stood with her back to them. Jana was already walking towards her.

Jeremiah and Peter rushed to catch up to her, Jeremiah's leg protesting the motion, but he ignored the pain. He was almost as transfixed as Jana at the sight of this place. Jana stopped short of the large platform, almost as if she feared getting too close. The men stopped beside her.

They looked up and saw the woman standing there slowly begin to turn around. When she was finally facing them, a smile spread across her porcelain face.

"Welcome home, little sister," she said, looking directly at Jana.

Chapter 10

Jana stood transfixed before this woman who had just called her 'Little Sister.' Jeremiah could see why. There was something about this woman that made it difficult to look away. She wasn't exactly beautiful in traditional terms. She wasn't tall. By his estimate, she couldn't be any taller than 5'4". She had long pitch-black hair that reached all the way down her back. She had it swept back behind her, but left it unbound, so Jeremiah could see it resting near her hips. She was slim and fit, but most of her physique was hidden behind what looked like a blue silk dress. It seemed to be made for someone a bit bigger than she was, as it also hid her feet from sight.

Jeremiah looked over at Peter. He seemed to be studying the woman in front of them, clearly un-phased by whatever quality was affecting both Jeremiah and Jana.

"Little sister?" Jana finally asked.

"Of course," the woman began, "You're a child of the sea, just like I am."

Jana's eyes lit up at those words. Jeremiah could see something there, something he had seen in her eyes when Peter had first offered to help her; he could see hope.

"What is a child of the sea?" Peter asked, unafraid.

The woman's eyes moved to look at Peter in an almost lazy manner, as if she didn't put any worth into the man asking the question.

"Tell me," the woman began, "What do you see when you look at me? What do you hear in this place?"

Peter screwed his face up in confusion at her question before answering, "I see a normal woman, late 20s, early 30s. I hear water dripping and echoing. I don't really understand your question or why it matters."

The woman turned her gaze back to Jana, "And what do you see, little sister? What do you hear?"

"Your skin, it isn't normal."

"No, it isn't. I have the skin of the sea, as do all of the children. Their people know it as their skin wrinkling when submerged for too long. But this is our natural state. We aren't made for the earth; we were made for the water. We're the stepping stone in humanity's evolution towards earth's greater portion."

"I don't understand, your skin looks normal to me," Jeremiah said, skeptically.

"Of course it does. You don't have the sight."

"Is this sounding even crazier than giant sea monsters to you, or am I finally feeling the blood loss of being shot?" Jeremiah asked Peter.

The woman narrowed her eyes at Jeremiah at those words. When she did so, Jeremiah felt he had no choice but to meet her gaze. His insides began to feel cold, his hands were suddenly clammy, and he felt like he was going to drown.

"Jeremiah? Are you okay?" Peter asked.

Jeremiah tried gasping for air and could feel himself falling into unconsciousness, when the woman finally tore her gaze away from him, and he could breathe again. He fell to his knees and gasped, letting oxygen flow into his body once again.

"What did you just do to him?" Peter demanded.

"Something you'll also feel if you don't maintain a tone of respect in your voice. I don't appreciate sarcasm at my expense."

Peter put his hand on Jeremiah's back as he tried to regain his composure. It had felt exactly like drowning. But that made no sense.

"Apologize, and we can keep this conversation going. Refuse and, well... I think you know."

"I'm sorry," Jeremiah let out, in between deep breaths.

The woman had a look on her face like she was pleased at her ability to make Jeremiah submit to her wishes. Jeremiah felt that it was something she took advantage of often.

"Now, then," she began, "What were we discussing? I lose my mind when I have too much fun, I'm afraid."

"You mentioned something you called 'the sight,'" Peter replied.

"Right," she said.

Jeremiah looked at Jana. Her eyes and her body hadn't moved an inch this entire time. She had the same look in her eyes. She was absolutely captivated by this woman. He wasn't sure there was anything that would break her concentration at this point.

"The sight is something special that we children have. Really, all five of our senses are special, but you asked why you see my skin as being 'normal,'" she used air quotes around the word, with a face that showed her disgust at its use.

"We can see things that you cannot. We can hear things you cannot. Feel, smell, taste, all of it. So when one of *you* lays their eyes on us, they see smooth skin. When one of our own looks upon us, they see the truth of who we are."

"That's why everyone dismissed Jana's concerns at her job," Jeremiah concluded.

"And it's why we allow some of our people to operate in the open. Unless you have the sight, you won't give us a second look. But those who do, we know they are one of us. And we watch them. We study them. We bring them home, as we have done with my little sister, here."

"But, how? How is any of that possible?" Peter asked, quizzically. Jeremiah could see that his interest was fully piqued, and he wanted to know more. He was just as engrossed as Jana, but in a much different way.

"I already told you. We're the next step in evolution. How does evolution happen? Genetic mutation. Over the entire time the earth has existed," she said.

"You're talking about over four billion years. Before humans even existed," Peter replied.

"Who said we're all human?" She replied, with a smirk, "Besides, humans weren't the first life forms, obviously. The mutation has been happening to every life form since life forms existed. Humans were just advanced enough to do something about it."

"How do you know these things? How are you so sure?" Peter asked.

The woman closed her eyes and smiled, "Because *They* tell us. Isn't that right, little sister?"

Jana simply nodded her head in agreement.

"You can hear them clearly now, can't you? Being closer to the ocean, closer to your family, it's woken you up."

"Who are *They*?" Peter asked, using the same inflection the woman had just used.

"*They* are the all-knowing ones. The true heirs of our world. The first life, and also the last," Jana whispered, barely loud enough for everyone to hear.

"That's right, little sister. They have spoken to us. Told us their tragic story and urged us to let them finally rise."

"So, what, these *They* things made your people evolve or something?" Peter asked. Jeremiah felt that Peter's curiosity was beginning to push it. He didn't want this woman to use whatever voodoo she had used on him on Peter. He wasn't sure his lungs could take it. Jeremiah put a hand on Peter's arm, motioning for him to calm down.

"That's right. They are powerful beyond measure. They have had a hand in everything, even trapped below the ocean, nothing could silence them," the inflection she and Jana had previously used was now gone. They now spoke of these beings more realistically than reverently.

"You said they told you their tragic story. What might that be?" Peter asked, having taken Jeremiah's silent advice to calm his voice, lest he raise this woman's ire.

"And why should I tell someone like you such a sacred tale?" the woman asked.

"You don't really have a reason to. I'm sure you have no intention of letting us leave this place, though. So, you have no reason not to either," Peter replied.

The woman's smirk turned serious just then, and Jeremiah looked at Peter to make sure he was still breathing normally. He was, which made Jeremiah breathe a sigh of relief.

"Alright, then. I'll tell you," she said, before taking a deep breath, "When the earth was in process of being created, they were there. They saw the stone and metals of the cosmos clash relentlessly, slowly building up what would become our universe, and our planet. They observed, but did not interfere, as they wanted nature to take its course. They were curious, as you are now. As the materials grew larger in size due to their cataclysmic nature, and our planet began to take form, it became harder and harder for them to keep their presence unfelt by the events taking place. Until, eventually, it became impossible.

"Once the motion was set and there was no way to change it, the materials began to collide with them. They weren't able to avoid this, and understanding that fact, they let it happen of their own volition. They allowed themselves to be struck by this cosmic material, until they were buried underneath it.

"That's right -- They have always been a part of our planet. Our earth's core was being formed, with layers of rock covering it. They were struck, and landed on that layer, and eventually, they were buried alive beneath millions of tons of earth. All they wanted was to watch our universe's birth, but they ended up being a part of it instead. Can you imagine a fate more tragic?

"But this process, it did not kill them. They could not die. They didn't even struggle. They accepted their fate and knew that it was an important one. So they slept.

They slept through much of the universe's life. They waited for something.

"Finally, that something happened. Life began to take form on our planet. The second something came alive, so did they. Their minds awoke while their bodies still slept, and their influence began to be felt by everything that was living. They are the reason the oceans filled with life. They were close to those beings that could breathe underwater and could approach them. But not all things accepted their presence or commands. They evolved in the other direction. Towards the land, towards the sky.

"But they would not be denied. As humans eventually developed, they reached out to us. Only a few were affected, and only a few accepted. But once they let them into their minds, it changed them. The ocean called to them, and they spent more time submerged, hoping for more signals from them. These subtle differences from the rest of their people allowed them to change in ways that the others could not. They began to feel more strongly and were eventually able to hear as well.

"As soon as it became strong enough in their genetics, they could hear the story of how they came to be here on earth. They told us that they knew they were here for a reason. That they were created to be here, and to guide them, their new people. Their children. They told us that we were drawn to them because we know, in the deepest part of our nature, that they are the ones meant to rule this world. They were meant to rise from the depths and show us the true way. That God created them as the true mirrors of his image, and we are simply the byproduct of their reflection.

"And so it is. Everything we have done was for them, to help them realize their destiny. Our collective destiny."

Jeremiah felt all of his preconceived ideals melt away at the sound of her fantastic tale. He didn't want to believe any of it, but he knew better. He knew those things were really here, and he knew they were at the bottom of the ocean. What reason did he have to not believe her story if he knows that the things that she talks about are real? It was getting harder and harder to be a skeptic.

He looked at his companions next to him. Peter had a deadpan look on his face, taking in all of the information that she had just laid out for them. Jana, however, had tears streaming down her face, as if she had just had a profound religious experience. In a manner of speaking, she had. She'd always seemed a bit odd, and Jeremiah was sure it wasn't just the impression that he got. He knew that many people had thought that about Jana throughout her life. There was a reason she was a grown woman and had nothing and no one to accompany her but her own neuroses. And she had finally found a place where she belongs, that makes sense to her. It must be a wonderful moment for her.

If only this happiness she felt didn't have dire implications for the rest of the world.

"What happens when they get here?" Peter asked, his eyes now on the floor beneath him.

The woman looked at him for a full minute before answering his question, "You die."

Without lifting his gaze, Peter asked another question, "Everyone? The whole world?"

"No. They've promised their children sanctuary from destruction. But the rest of you will feel the cataclysm that created this world in the first place. This is their promised penance for their four-billion-year imprisonment. You will be buried in the rock and metal that buried them for so long. And then, the world will continue on without you. As if you never even existed. And I know the reason you two wanted to seek us out.

And the answer to your question is... No. There's nothing that can be done to stop them now."

Jeremiah watched Peter's expression slowly fade into reluctant acceptance. As if all of his will to go on had just been taken from him. Jeremiah felt the same emotions in him. They had thought they could be heroes of some sort and stop these things that had killed his wife. They hadn't stopped to consider that maybe it was an impossible task. Because doing that would mean the end of hope for them all.

"Why?" Jeremiah asked.

"I don't like to repeat my-" She was cut off by Jeremiah.

"Why did my wife have to die for your beliefs? And the crew she was supposed to go with? Innocent people! Good people!" Jeremiah was shouting now. He felt cheated. He knew his wife had been cheated out of her life. All because these radical people wanted to please their deity, or whatever they wanted to call them.

"Was it easy for you? To condemn all of these people to die because you think they're inferior?"

The woman had a bored expression on her face. She clearly wasn't amused by Jeremiah's shouting.

"How did you even do it? Replace that whole crew without anyone noticing?" Jeremiah demanded. He still needed answers.

"We didn't replace the *entire* crew," She replied, now in a mocking tone, "Just a few key members. We have people everywhere. People with the expertise to carry out the mission. People who can kill professionally. People who can make some very convincing masks. Really, we're a pool of talented individuals. It was a lot easier than you think. Both pulling it off and giving the order to kill your wife."

Jeremiah saw red at that, "Why you-" he couldn't continue his oncoming expletive, as she had once again seized him in a drowning sensation. He grabbed at his throat and struggled against her.

"Of course, I don't really remember which one your wife was. They're all the same to me," she replied, "And just because I *know* what you were about to call me, maybe I should tell you what to call me."

She released him again, this time he was able to stay on his feet as he regained his breathing.

"My name is Layla Salem. You'll call me Madam Salem, if you know what's good for you," she looked across the room to the entrance and shouted, "Little brother Wilson, take these two and put them

186

somewhere where they can think about everything I've told them."

Not a second after the words left her mouth, Jeremiah heard the stone wall behind him moving to allow the one they'd met before and one other accompanying him into the chamber. They quickly walked towards them, each one grabbing one of them by the arm. Jeremiah was grabbed by the one they hadn't met yet. His grip was hard, and it wouldn't be an easy grip to break, even if he wanted to try.

Jeremiah looked to Peter and saw him wince in pain from Andrew's grip on his bicep. Peter was more fragile than Jeremiah was, being as sick as he is. Jeremiah felt a sting of pity for the pain Peter must be feeling.

They were turned around and led away from Madam Salem's room without another word. No motion was made for Jana to also leave, and Jeremiah assumed that she had more to discuss with Madam Salem.

The two men walked without any protest. They now knew that any resistance would be futile. Jeremiah felt that even if he wanted to escape, there'd be no way he could find his way out anyway. Their current situation was truly a hopeless one.

They crossed the threshold out of Madam Salem's room, and the rock behind them slid back into place, blocking out the light from inside. They were once again in pitch black darkness, blinding them to any of their surroundings.

"Jeremiah..." he heard Peter whisper.

"Yeah?"

"...I'm sorry."

Chapter 11

Hours later, and Jeremiah's vision had finally adjusted as much as it was probably going to. He could see the confines of his makeshift prison cell. He sat inside with Peter, both of them sitting on opposite sides of it. It looked like someone had gone to some painstaking effort in order to make this room actually look like a cell. A grid of bars with a door built into them was shoved into the stone at the top and the bottom. Jeremiah had no idea what kind of strength or how many people were required to make this. He could see only the wall across from them and down the opposite side of the hallway, for lack of a better term, and it was clear that the cell they resided in was the only one they had. They must not expect many prisoners. That wasn't entirely surprising. Genocidal psychopaths aren't known for taking prisoners.

Jeremiah and Peter had hardly spoken since they were led here and locked up. There wasn't much to say between them. There were no more plans to be made or hopes to be discussed. Likely, they'd sit here until the day of reckoning arrived and they were murdered by giant sea monsters. Peter had had a coughing fit when they finally sat down, and Jeremiah had tried to help calm him down. By the sound of it, Peter's lungs weren't taking the news of their impending demise very well.

Jeremiah rested his head against the wall behind him. He wondered if anything they had done in the last few days had made any sort of difference in any meaningful way. He wondered if his wife's soul was any more at rest now than it had been the morning before all of this craziness found its way into his world. She had always been the one who wanted excitement. How ironic that the excitement that found her also made its way to him. And it looked like it would be ending in the same way as it did for her.

"Do you think they feed prisoners?" Jeremiah asked, as he felt his stomach knot in hunger.

"I'm not sure if they have a prisoner keeping protocol here."

"I wouldn't think so."

"I'm sorry, Jeremiah."

"I don't think I can blame you for their culinary shortcomings, Peter."

"You know what I mean."

"It doesn't matter, man. There were only two ways this was going to play out, no matter what. Either I would've died when those things finally came up from the water without ever knowing what happened to my wife, without ever having anything even resembling closure, or I die knowing everything. No matter what, I was going to die. And so were you, and so was everyone else. At least I don't have to die ignorant of the facts. This is better, I think. I only ever wrote about adventures or taught kids how to write adventures, kind of. This time, I lived one. A short one, and it doesn't exactly have a happy ending, but it's better than nothing."

Peter fell silent. Jeremiah was telling the truth, though. He really meant everything he said. He was happier for knowing what he now knew. Maybe Sasha was more at rest now, happy that her dull husband had finally lived a little and had had some remarkable experiences. Getting shot, blowing up what was probably a federal agent, and going to sea world probably weren't in everyone else's definition of 'remarkable experiences' though.

"Do you think Jana is going to be okay?" Peter asked.

"Probably. You heard that Salem lady. They seem to be pretty into the concept of family down here, and they consider Jana family. I think she's going to be fine. You don't have to apologize to *her*. This is probably the best thing that could have happened to her."

"I suppose so. It kind of sucks that she turned on us so quickly, though."

"Don't think of it that way. That lady has some weird hypnotic thing over the rest of them. There's no way Jana could have resisted. I don't exactly blame her, you know?"

"I know. I guess I don't either. But I had been hoping that somehow, all three of us would make it out of here alive. At this point, that's like wishing my lung cancer would magically disappear," Peter said as he chuckled. That chuckle brought with it another coughing fit.

"It's getting worse," Jeremiah said, after a moment.

"Well, you know how cancer gets."

This time, Jeremiah let out a small chuckle. Peter's sense of humor was finally surfacing, which was an unfortunate choice of words to think. For the first time since they met, they knew their future. Nothing was unclear, and in a strange way, he thought that it was relaxing them. Finally allowing them to let their guard down. Something about the certainty of their deaths was freeing.

"I suppose there's no way any of your connections can get us out of this one, huh?" Jeremiah asked.

Peter reached into his pocket and pulled out his cell phone. He pressed the power button and the light from the screen was practically blinding to Jeremiah, even though he was all the way across the room. How did he even still have his phone? He remembered that no one had searched him, but he hadn't had anything in his pockets but his wallet. He had figured that someone would've checked Peter.

"No reception underneath all this rock. So, to answer your question, no. No connections for us down here," Peter said before locking the phone and returning it to his pocket. As soon as he did, he let out a sigh of frustration, "I should not have done that. Now I have to wait for my eyes to adjust to the dark again. I hate being this blind."

"They didn't search you and take your phone?" Jeremiah asked.

"No. Why would they? Phones wouldn't work down here. What good would it do me?"

"Light..." Jeremiah whispered.

"What?"

"Light! It has light! We can use it to find our way through these tunnels!" Jeremiah exclaimed.

"I think you're forgetting the fact that we're stuck in this prison. Light can't help us in here. Except to give our eyes a hard time."

"What if we found a way out?"

"Then, that'd be a different story. But I don't see that happening. Not unless one of them comes to feed us and we trick them like in some old TV show. But, again, I don't see that happening. These guys seem obsessed with not upsetting their 'Mistress' or 'Madam' or whatever they call her."

Jeremiah stood, using the wall for support, and walked over to the door to their cell. He felt around it for a while, until he located the lock. It wasn't a complicated one, and he felt confident that he could open it if he had the right tools to do so.

"You wouldn't happen to have a lockpicking kit on you, would you?" Jeremiah asked.

"No, why would I carry that around with me?"

"I was just hoping against hope, I suppose."

"We lost, Jeremiah. It's over. We tried, we tried our best, and we just... we lost. I think it's time to throw in the towel and hope this rock cell becomes a little more comfortable the longer we're in here."

Jeremiah heard his stomach growl. It didn't feel like that would be happening, especially given his hunger. More likely, they'd starve to death. Well, depending on how much longer the wait for those things was.

Jeremiah didn't want to sit down. His stomach knotted up less when he was standing. Plus, standing was somehow soothing the ache in his thigh from the bullet wound. Looks like he probably wasn't going to be able to attend an anti-gun rally like he jokingly thought he would.

The light from Peter's phone had affected his sight as well. He could only see a foot or two in front of his face. It left him wishing he hadn't inquired about him calling someone for help. Just then, he felt a presence behind him. He turned around, but it was pointless, he couldn't make out any features.

"Hello?" Jeremiah asked, "Who's there?"

There was silence for a moment, before someone finally spoke, "It's me."

"Jana?" Peter asked from behind Jeremiah. He could hear Peter stand up.

"Yeah. Hey guys," she replied.

"What are you doing here?" Jeremiah replied, obviously shocked.

"I wanted to apologize. This... this has been so great. I've met so many people these past few hours. So many people who treated me like family. And called me things like 'little sister.' But I left you guys out to dry, so to speak."

"We talked about that," Peter said, "And we understand. We don't blame you for what happened back there."

"...Thank you," Jana said, almost whispering, "I've wanted this for so long. I've wanted to belong somewhere for so long. This is a dream come true. But..." her voice trailed off.

"But?" Jeremiah asked.

"But I can't have my dream at the expense of everyone else in the world. No matter how much they've treated me like a weirdo, or like I didn't belong, they don't deserve to die. Especially you two. You don't deserve to rot in a cell. Everyone deserves to be warned."

"What are you saying?" Peter asked.

"I'm saying, we're leaving. Right now."

"Jana, are you sure? They won't let you come back if you do this. They might try to kill you. They could catch us," Jeremiah said.

"I'm sure," she replied, "And Jeremiah, you're staying here."

"Wait, *what*?!" Jeremiah exclaimed.

"Shhh," Jana silenced Jeremiah, "Your leg. We need to move quickly, and you can't do that with your injury. Peter's lungs are compromised, but he can still move fast. You have to wait here. As soon as we're out, we have to call someone and tell them about this place. As soon as they come and search it, they'll let you out. Right now, we have to focus on getting Peter and I out of here."

"Why don't you just go by yourself and call someone, then?" Peter asked.

"Think about it. If I call and say that I found some crazy fish people's hideout, do you think they'll come? But if Peter Jacobson calls, they'll rush here to arrest you within the hour. Even if I called to tell them I knew where you are, they won't rush as fast as if you called yourself. It's the fastest way to get us help."

"She makes a good point," Jeremiah said, "Alright. I'll wait here."

"Okay," Jana said. That was followed by the sound of keys fumbling and the door in front of him unlocking. Jeremiah stepped as far from where he knew the door was to make room for Peter to walk through.

"How did you get those keys?" Peter asked, before adding, "You know what, I don't want to know. Let's just get out of here."

Jeremiah heard the cell door close, Peter presumably now free.

"You'll be out of here in no time, Jeremiah. I promise," Peter said, before Jeremiah heard their footsteps as they ran away from the cell.

"I'll be waiting," Jeremiah whispered to himself.

***

"Aren't they going to hear us running?" Peter asked, as he and Jana were enacting their escape.

"No, they're all asleep."

"Footsteps are loud in here, and we're running. There's no way this won't wake them up."

"Don't worry, they sleep submerged in water. By the time they notice something is off, it'll be too late. Your cell wasn't too far from the entrance. It's just about finding your way."

Jana was dragging Peter along by the hand. Without her, he'd definitely be lost by now, possibly forever. He had no idea which way they were going, but he hoped that they'd be at the entrance as soon as possible. He could feel his lungs protesting all of this movement. If they can't hear footsteps, they'll sure as hell hear him coughing his lungs out. *Keep it together, keep it together*, he told himself.

"We're almost there," Jana said as they continued to rush.

Suddenly, Jana stopped running.

"What's wrong?" Peter asked.

"Uh. There's a guard. And he's looking right at us."

"What?!" Peter exclaimed.

Just then, he heard the sound of people fighting, but he couldn't see any of it. He knew it was to his left somewhere, but he was afraid of trying to intervene. If he threw a punch, he was just as likely to hit Jana as he was to hit the guard.

A few moments passed, and all Peter could hear was the sound of struggling. He hoped Jana was able to hold her own, or this escape would be the shortest in history. He heard a masculine grunt in the darkness, and suddenly someone grabbed his hand and dragged him forward.

"Jana?" Peter asked.

"Yeah, it's me. He alerted the rest of them, but the exit is right up ahead."

"How did you...?"

"Poked him in the eyes. Punched him in the kidney. Kicked him in the groin," she said, as if it wasn't anything serious.

"Are you serious?" Peter asked.

"I took self-defense. Well, I watched videos."

Obviously, they had paid off.

The next time they abruptly stopped running, Peter could feel his lungs start to swell up in anticipation of a coughing fit. Jana was obviously able to see him.

"Just let it out, Peter. We're already on the elevator. They can't stop us now."

As soon as she said those words, he let out a loud cough that echoed in his chest and caused him a lot of pain. He coughed for a few seconds as he felt themselves being lifted upwards, out of the darkness of this cave.

The darkness that surrounded them within the cave was banished when the platform hiding the elevator moved, and they could see the appearing sun. By the looks of it, it wouldn't be so bright for much longer. The sun was setting. It was probably around 5 or 6 in the afternoon at this point. They had been down there much longer than they had thought.

"Do you have your phone?" Jana asked.

"Yeah, in my pocket," he said as he pulled it out.

"Well, what are you waiting for? Make the call!"

Peter nodded and unlocked his phone. With no time to waste, he quickly dialed 911 and hit the call button. After a moment, a woman on the other end answered.

"911, what's your emergency?"

"This is Peter Jacobson. I'm on the government's most wanted list. I am currently at La Jolla Shores, underneath the pier. I know they have to send people after me, trace this phone if you have to, but send someone here now. I found the Children of the Sea."

There was silence from the other end for a few moments after that. Peter was starting to worry that she didn't believe him or that maybe there were no government contacts through the emergency lines. After a minute of worrying, he heard a new voice. Still female, but more commanding.

"Mr. Jacobson. We've sent fifteen agents to your position. We're tracing your phone call. But I have to ask... why would you give yourself away?"

"Because I had to. It's the Children of the Sea, ma'am. I know you know who I'm talking about. When your men get here, tell them not to shoot me. I have to show them how to get inside. Bring flashlights. And, ma'am?"

"Yes?"

"You might need more than fifteen. I have no idea how many there are."

"Understand, Mr. Jacobson, that once this is taken care of, you *will* be arrested and you *will* be imprisoned," the woman said.

"I understand. But this is more important. Hurry, please. They already know I've escaped."

There was a click as the woman on the other end of the phone hung up. That was it, then. That was all that they could do. All that was left was to wait for the Feds to show up and hopefully clean up the mess underground. Peter prayed, the irony of which wasn't lost on him, that someone showed up to help before they caught up to them above ground. And before they hurt Jeremiah.

***

It hadn't been more than three minutes when Jeremiah heard rushed footfalls outside of his cell. He tried to count how many people were running past, but it was impossible because of all of the echoes that accompanied them. He just knew there were a lot of them.

It hadn't taken long for them to figure out that Peter had escaped, it seems. It hadn't taken long for them to start going after them either. It didn't look like any of them were stopping to check on him. He figured they glanced into his cell and saw that he was still in there and gave it no more thought. That was good, but it also meant that they were going after Peter and Jana en masse.

A minute later, the footsteps and echoes ceased. They must all have gone too far from his cell. Or maybe they caught up to them. He couldn't hear anything else, but he began to worry. His eyes were nowhere near adjusting to the darkness of his cell, as he sat down against the wall. So he didn't see it when Madam Salem approached his cell.

"This is a strange feeling," she said.

Jeremiah flinched at the sound of her voice. He hadn't expected anyone to talk to him right then, "What?"

"Someone betraying us. Someone choosing you people over their own family. It's a strange feeling."

"Someone not wanting to join your genocidal crusade confuses you?" Jeremiah asked, his heart racing from the scare.

"Someone not wanting to be accepted by people who are just like them confuses me. Why in the world would she choose to help your little sick friend over being a part of something greater?"

Jeremiah couldn't see her, but he knew that she probably looked genuinely confused at this turn of events. That in itself confused him.

"We would've loved her, protected her, sheltered her, given her a home. And we made sure she knew that. What is it about you inferior humans that called to her more strongly than the call of the sea? The call of the heirs?"

"I can't answer that," Jeremiah said, solemnly. He really considered Madam Salem's question. He didn't understand what drove Jana to help them when she could have had everything she ever wanted. Had he been in her position, he wasn't sure that he would've made the difficult decision that she made. Hell, he felt that he probably would have stayed with his new family and lived happily ever after. It made his admiration of Jana grow stronger, that she was able to do something like that.

"I guess it doesn't matter at this point. The heirs will rise, no matter what. I don't know exactly what your friends plan to do, but it won't change a thing. All they've done is ruin humanity's chance of moving forward."

"What do you mean?" Jeremiah asked.

"People are coming. They're going to find us. They're going to exterminate us. And with our people dead, nothing will be left of humanity. And that is all thanks to you and your friends. We were going to evolve under their rule. And now... we're all going to go extinct."

"Do you really think that they were going to let you and your people live?" Jeremiah asked.

"Of course," she said without hesitation, "We are their children. They protect their children. I have no doubt that we would have prospered."

"I guess we'll never know, now," Jeremiah said.

Madam Salem didn't reply to his last statement. Everything fell silent. Jeremiah could still feel her presence outside of his cell. He knew she was standing there. His sight began to return and he could see the outline of her body. Her posture looked firm. She was as sure of herself as ever. He wondered why she wasn't killing him, but felt that if he asked her that, it would convince her to do the thing he feared.

Gunshots went off somewhere deeper in the cave. Jeremiah jerked his head to look in the direction he heard them coming from, but he saw nothing. When he turned to look at Madam Salem again, her posture hadn't changed at all. She's accepted her fate, it seems. Much as he had resolved to do not long before Jana rescued Peter.

Gunshots continued, and neither of them said a word. They both knew that Peter and Jana had succeeded in their mission. It was only a matter of time before they reached Jeremiah's cell. Jeremiah wondered what would happen after everything was done here. He had no ideas. He just knew that he'd be free soon, and these people would be gone from the world. The thought gave Jeremiah a somber feeling.

"Madam Salem, we have to go," Andrew said. Jeremiah hadn't even been aware that he was there as well.

"No. It's over, little brother."

The gunshots got closer until Jeremiah could see light approaching his cell. It was almost time. A few seconds later, he saw someone in what resembled

SWAT gear holding a flashlight and an automatic rifle walk into his field of vision.

"Get on the ground!" he shouted at Madam Salem and Andrew.

With light now illuminating his surroundings, Jeremiah looked at her. Her position still did not change, and her expression was one of someone who sure that they were in the right, there was no changing their mind. She even had a little smirk on her face. Andrew stood next to her, posturing in a protective way.

"I said get on the ground!" the man shouted again. He was wearing a visor over his eyes, so Jeremiah didn't know if Madam Salem could even affect him the way she had affected Jeremiah earlier.

Madam Salem and Andrew didn't comply with his wishes, and he opened fire on them. Gunshots rang out throughout what seemed like the entire cave, almost deafening in their intensity. As if in slow motion, Jeremiah watched their bodies fall limply to the ground. He felt as though their bodies hitting the stone would have made a noise, had the gunshots that preceded it not left him with ringing in his ears.

The SWAT officer approached his cell soon after and addressed him, "Are you alright?" he asked.

"...yeah," Jeremiah responded, slightly shell shocked. This was the second time he's watched someone die right before his eyes in the last few days.

The SWAT officer shot the lock to Jeremiah's cell, allowing it to swing open. Jeremiah noticed for the first time that the cell door opened inward. Little details were overtaking him, as if attempting to shield him from the horror of his situation.

The SWAT officer walked towards Jeremiah and offered him a hand to help him stand up. Jeremiah complied and came to his feet, then slowly walked out of his cell, the SWAT officer behind him. As soon as he stepped out, he felt a hand grab his ankle. It was Madam Salem, still clinging to life.

"This changes nothing. They're coming. They'll be here in two days. And you can't stop them," she said.

And with that, the SWAT officer shot Madam Salem in the head, putting her down once and for all.

Jeremiah's ears began ringing again. Some of her blood got on his clothes. Jeremiah didn't know how to process everything that had just happened. Without a word, the SWAT officer directed Jeremiah down the hallway, and they walked for a while.

Jeremiah's mind wasn't on the situation anymore. He felt as though he had receded back into the recesses of his mind, trying to keep himself from breaking down. He noticed little flares leading the way back to the exit of the cave.

Soon, they were on the elevator. Jeremiah could vaguely hear the SWAT officer report something into his walkie-talkie. The elevator began to rise.

Chapter 12

The sun was setting. Jeremiah blinked his eyes several times, unsure if he could believe his vision. He was outside. He had made it out. Somehow.

He looked out around him. Parked all around the shore were black cars with tinted windows and two SWAT team vans. Further away, he could see the parking lot was full of white vans which he could vaguely see had news channel logos on them. There's a lot to be said for how seriously their government takes the arrest of someone on their most wanted list, and how quickly the media can nip at their heels. There were cops and federal agents standing around, talking amongst themselves. But Jeremiah felt that most of them were in the cave, doing to the rest of those people what one of them had done to Madam Salem and Andrew. He still couldn't get her last words out of his head. Two days... That was so soon.

The SWAT officer began to walk away when Jeremiah snapped out of it and stopped him by grabbing his arm.

"Excuse me, where's Peter? Er, Mr. Jacobson?" Jeremiah asked.

"He's in custody, inside one of the vans. As soon as we're done here, we're taking him in," the officer replied.

"Can I talk to him?" Jeremiah asked.

The SWAT officer looked at him for a moment before nodding his head and motioning for Jeremiah to follow him. Jeremiah walked through the wet sand, following the officer to one of the SWAT vans parked on the shore. He wondered if his leg would ever stop hurting. As soon as they approached the van, the SWAT officer stopped him.

"Five minutes. Then we're having someone take you away from this location. We don't want you trying to rescue your friend here, being an adventurer that you are and all."

Jeremiah was a bit surprised at this, "I'm not being arrested as well?"

"Why would you be? Mr. Jacobson confessed to everything, including kidnapping you, forcing you to do his bidding against your will, and threatening you with a bomb that he then used to kill a federal agent. All we'd need from you is a testimony, but I doubt it'll be necessary to put him away forever."

Jeremiah was shocked. Peter had taken the complete fall and had absolved Jeremiah's name of any blame. He was in the clear. Not that it really mattered, though. It didn't change anything, like Madam Salem had said.

The SWAT officer opened the back of the van, and Jeremiah saw Peter sitting in there, his hands cuffed behind his back. That couldn't be comfortable. And it was probably difficult for him to breathe in that position. Peter looked over at him and smirked. The officer then motioned for Jeremiah to get inside of the van.

"Luckily, he's cuffed and weak, he won't be a threat to you in there with him. But I'll be standing out here. If anything happens, just shout, and I'll put him down," the officer said.

Jeremiah nodded and got into the van. The officer closed the van doors behind him and he heard the sound of a lock. Jeremiah sat down opposite Peter and sighed.

"Well, I guess we kind of did it, huh?" Jeremiah asked.

"In a manner of speaking. I told them that they have to warn everyone about what's about to happen."

"And what did they say?"

"They told me not to worry about that. That the government would take care of it. I don't think they're in a hurry to disclose a whole lot of information to me, given my track record," Peter replied.

"I can see that. So, you confessed to everything, huh?" Jeremiah asked.

"Yeah. They told me the name of the federal agent I killed."

"What was it?"

Peter looked solemnly at Jeremiah before answering, "You don't want that information in your head, Jeremiah. Knowing his name only makes it more difficult to live with. Trust me on that."

Jeremiah nodded. He understood. Madam Salem's death had had a bigger effect on him than that federal agent. Maybe because he'd known her name, or maybe because it happened in a much less incendiary situation, he didn't exactly know. But he knew it would be weighing heavily on him for a while. However long that was.

"No more escape plans?" Jeremiah asked.

"I don't think so. I think I'm stuck in this one. But it's okay. My life for the kingdom, right?"

"That's not the right expression," Jeremiah replied with a chuckle.

"I was trying to give it a personal touch. That's why I'm not a writer, I suppose," Peter said.

"What now?" Jeremiah asked.

"Now... you do whatever you want to do. They said they know how long it'll be before those things show up and start trying to destroy us. So, wait for them to tell you what to do, I guess. You could ask before they take you home, but I somehow doubt they'll be too forthcoming with information, seeing as you're a civilian and all."

"And you go to prison."

"I don't think I'm going to prison. I'm pretty sure I'm being taken to some kind of federal holding cell somewhere. I don't even think they intend to give me a trial, given the severity of what I did. Or, rather, what I tried to do. For all of our efforts, we didn't even get a chance to warn the populace," Peter said, sadness in his voice.

"After what we heard down there... I'm not sure it would have made a difference," Jeremiah responded.

"Maybe you're right."

There was a knock on the van door followed by the SWAT officer shouting, "Wrap it up. We're taking the civilians home."

Jeremiah turned to Peter with a puzzled look on his face, "Civilians? Plural?" he asked.

"Yeah, they're taking Jana home, too. She's lucky. I'm the only one of us who got manhandled by one of these guys," Peter said, laughter returning to his voice.

"I hope you'll be okay, Peter. Thank you for helping me find some closure. And thank you for the adventure," Jeremiah said, sincerely.

"You're welcome, Jeremiah. And, again, I'm sorry it all went so wrong."

Jeremiah nodded, then knocked on the van door to be let out. The SWAT officer quickly unlocked the doors, opened them, and helped Jeremiah climb out of the van. Jeremiah gave Peter one last glance before walking away, and they nodded at each other knowingly. They had given it their best shot. That's really all that can be asked of them in the end.

***

A few hours later, Peter was on his way to wherever they meant to stash him until the end of days. Luckily for him, it didn't seem to be too far off anyway. He hadn't seen what happened, but he heard a lot of it. They had apparently killed everyone in the caves. No one was willing to comply with them, and they had been left no choice but to open fire. So that settled it. There was only one 'Child of the Sea' left and it was Jana. At least it was someone who still had their sanity.

Peter was still in the back of a SWAT van but was now accompanied by one officer sitting across from him, with his gun at the ready. He didn't know what kind of resistance they expected from a man with stage three cancer, but it was nice to know that the government was at least trying to be diligent.

"Any idea where they're taking me?" Peter asked.

The SWAT officer did not respond. Peter had expected as much. But it didn't sound like he would have to wait much longer to see his new permanent home. The van was slowing down and making motions like it was parking somewhere.

Peter's suspicions were proven correct when the SWAT officer in front of him stood up, unlocked the van doors and stepped out. They had reached their destination.

A different officer reached inside and grabbed Peter by the arm to make him leave the van. Not exactly the help he had wanted exiting, but it would have to do, he supposed.

He looked around and saw that they were in a parking garage occupied solely by vehicles you'd imagine federal agents driving. In another life, maybe he would've been working with the government instead of against it and would be driving around in one of these things. No use pondering what-ifs, though. What's done is done.

The SWAT officer pulled him by the arm towards their left, where Peter could see double doors that probably led to some kind of high security federal jail. When the doors opened, Peter found that he couldn't have been more wrong.

He saw lines of computer monitors with people in suits in front of them, all of them working diligently towards some unnamed task. Ahead of them, he saw an office, which is where they were headed. He was in a building full of analysts and probably some government higher-ups. He would have asked why they were there, but he knew he'd be met with the same silence and elected to just wait until it was explained to him by someone with more authority.

They walked past, and none of the analysts gave him a second look. They were all completely engrossed in their duties. It was admirable to see, but he felt a little jilted that no one was paying attention to him. He was used to having all eyes and ears on him or looking for him, that it was only a little insulting to be so ignored, even while being walked in a pair of handcuffs.

Soon, they reached the office that Peter had seen when they walked in. There was a small cell inside of the office, and Peter knew that would be where he would be deposited. He was right, as the officer walked in front of him, opened the cell and motioned for him to walk inside. Peter complied, and as soon as he was in the cell, the officer removed his handcuffs and locked the door behind him.

Peter sat down on a bench inside of the cell and watched as the SWAT officer walked away. He was now alone in this office. Peter started wondered why they had put him there and left him all alone. He took a look around and saw two desks. One directly in front of him and the other to his right. Both of the desks faced him so he couldn't see anything on the computer monitors situated on top of them. He knew they were placed this way so whoever was sitting at those desks could also keep an eye on him. He couldn't help but feel that this cell was designed for criminals far more dangerous than he was.

Before long, a tall African-American woman in a suit walked in through the doors that Peter had been walked through to reach this office. She took a look at Peter and slowly walked towards him. Something about this woman's gait was both menacing and endearing.

"Peter Jacobson," she said. Peter immediately recognized her voice as the one he had spoken to on the phone earlier.

"That's me," Peter replied.

"I'll cut to the chase here. My name is Felicia Fletcher. I was the woman put in charge of finding you when we discovered you were trying to expose some of our more... important secrets. You killed one of my best men. But, in spite of that, you *did* lead us right to the people we'd been looking for since before you caught a big whiff of a juicy story to post on the internet. So, thank you for that."

"You're welcome."

"That being said, you're still going to rot in a cell, much like the one you're currently in, for the rest of your life," Felicia said.

"That's probably not as long as you think it'll be," Peter replied.

"Yes, we know all about your cancer, but it isn't going to buy you any mercy here."

"No, not the cancer. Those things. They're coming, and they're coming soon. It's already been a year and three months. They have to be closing in. It could be any day now."

Felicia laughed, "Mr. Jacobson, you have nothing to worry about when it comes to those things. See, we've developed some weapons that can easily bring them down and keep all of our people safe. They're very accurate as well, so there isn't even a need to evacuate or cause any panic. It'll be over before the public even knows what's happening."

"You're wrong," Peter replied.

"Excuse me?"

"Those things... they can survive whatever you throw at them. While we were in the caves, those people told us what those things are. They've been alive for billions of years. They were buried underneath meteors. They've been on this planet as long as its existed, Ms. Fletcher. I know you think you can kill them... but I'm telling you, I don't think you can."

"And what makes you such an expert? You listened to the stories of some insane people living in a wet cave, and you think that means you know what these things can and can't survive?" Felicia asked.

"I... I just have this feeling in my gut... that they weren't lying. You have to tell everyone to evacuate. You have to get the people to safety, you--" Peter was cut off.

"I don't have to do anything you say. You're a prisoner here, Jacobson. You're a criminal. I don't have to listen to you. I know what our military is capable of. And even if that wasn't enough, we have the cooperation of every military force in the world. You think you understand what's happening because of cave people, but we've been monitoring this situation for over a year. We know they're almost here. And we know where they'll be showing up, and we know how many there are," Felicia was getting angrier.

"How many are there?" Peter asked.

"We've counted twelve. And from what we've seen, they're going to be rising all over the Pacific Ocean, with most of them coming up on the east coast of Asia, and everywhere in between there and our west coast. All of the world's military forces are aware, and they're all going to be attacking with these new weapons. So, like I said, it'll be over before anyone knows what happened."

Peter grew silent. He wanted to believe that it would work. But he couldn't shake the feeling in his gut telling him that it wouldn't. That nothing they did was going to stop what was coming.

"I hope you're right, Ms. Fletcher," Peter said, "So what are you going to do with me?"

"Nothing. You're all but useless to us now. You weren't able to 'blow the lid' off of this secret, and we're still proceeding exactly as we had planned. You failed. We're just going to hold you here until it's all over. Then we'll hand you over to the California state government and let them handle your incarceration and trial," Felicia said.

"So, I'm just here to make sure I don't get in the way between now and when everything happens?"

"Exactly. We'll also be keeping a close eye on that friend of yours, Jeremiah Wilkins. We know you forced him into doing some reprehensible things, but he still learned information he shouldn't have. We'll have people following him and watching him. If he does anything to compromise our plans, we'll kill him. Let's hope he's smart."

"I know how you all are about keeping your secrets. Why wouldn't you just lock him up like you've done to me? Or kill him? I know you lot aren't above doing that to someone. I've seen your dirty laundry," Peter said.

"Let's just say, there isn't enough hush money in the right pockets for us to be able to make Mr. Wilkins disappear. The press caught wind of what happened at the beach. Hell, they were there for most of it. As much as we wanted to be covert with this, we needed the manpower. You can't mobilize people like that without newspapers and reporters following you. Your friend is somewhat of a celebrity around the newsroom water coolers. 'The man who was kidnapped by Peter Jacobson and forced to save us from a cult' and all that. We get rid of him; they'll level some questions we don't want to answer. Letting him live and keeping an eye on him was the easiest solution. Unless, like I said, he tried to compromise our plan. And, in the process, make our lives much more difficult."

"So that's it? That's what decides a human life for you people? Convenience? I suppose you'd let those things kill everyone if that was *convenient* for you, wouldn't you?"

"I don't think you're in a position to judge anyone for how they decide who lives and who dies. Was he your first kill?" Felicia asked.

Peter didn't answer. He just hung his head as he was once again reminded of what he had done.

"What about Jana?" Peter asked after a moment of silence.

"She's been asked to help our scientists understand what makes her different. She'll be compensated, since she seems to have done nothing wrong. And she's in the same situation as your dear friend Jeremiah. The media loves her and wants her safe. She's much less likely to talk while she's complying with us and being paid for it, so it works for us. Is your mind at ease now?"

Peter remained silent. Internally, he was relieved that it seemed the two people he had dragged into his world were going to be okay. But he was tempering that emotion, unsure if he could trust Felicia's word.

"I don't actually care. But I have to ask... you knew we would eventually catch up to you. Why not leave the country? You have connections, friends, dirt on the right people. You could've gotten all of this done from far away. It seems like a lapse in judgment. The cancer hasn't spread to your brain, has it?"

"What I've known for a long time is that I'm dying. I had an expiration date hanging over my head since before I made your most wanted list. You think I wanted to spend my last days behind a computer screen, watching this all go down from a small house in Finland? No, I wanted to be here. I wanted to see everything myself. I wanted to die doing what I was put on this planet to do."

"And what might that be, Mr. Jacobson?" Felicia asked.

"Keeping you and your bosses honest."

"That'll be hard to do from a prison cell. But I certainly hope you enjoy watching us defend humanity from in there. We'll, of course, be monitoring the activity. And you'll be able to see some of it on our screens from in here. The governments will be the heroes, and no one will care about Peter Jacobson."

He wanted to believe he had made some kind of difference leading up to all of these events. And he remembered that he had. Jeremiah had gotten closure, or some semblance of it, thanks to him. Peter looked down at the ground before him and hoped that Jeremiah would keep himself safe and not do anything rash. In their last conversation, they had come to the conclusion that there was nothing more to be done. That warning people might not have actually done anything for anyone. Hopefully he kept believing that and just left everything alone.

"Get comfortable, Mr. Jacobson. It's going to be an interesting few days," Felicia said, already walking away from Peter.

***

After what was somehow only the second most uncomfortable car ride of the day, Jana stood once more in front of her home. The questions that had been burning in her mind for so long finally had answers. She now knew why she was so strange and why strange events had been happening around her.

But these answers did nothing to comfort her. She had found a new community. People to call her own. People that would have accepted her. And she sold them out. Her new family. Her new, insane and extremist family.

With a sigh, Jana walked to her front door, undid the many locks she would eventually remove, and walked inside. Once the door was shut behind her, Jana collapsed onto the floor and wept.

After all of these answers, Jana was left with more dire questions: What now? The Children of the Sea had said that once the true gods emerged, only they would remain at their side. If Jana was one of them, would she survive the coming events? Would they know that she betrayed them and exact revenge? Or was there never any chance of anyone surviving their emergence?

And the most important question of all: Does any of this even matter?

After a few minutes, Jana collected herself and walked to her kitchen. She opened numerous drawers, looking for something that she may not even have. But it wasn't long before her hands closed around a book of matches. She shoved them in her pocket and walked back outside with a sense of purpose she'd rarely felt.

On the side of her house, she found a garden hose that would fit her intention perfectly. It was long, more than long enough for what she needed. Jana unscrewed the hose from the faucet and rolled it up to carry it over to her car. Once there, she inserted one end of the hose into her gas tank and walked the rest of it inside, careful not to pull it out of her car as she did so.

She had never tried syphoning gas before, but it seemed like it'd be simple from what she'd read about it before. If the fiction she'd read was to be believed, all she had to do was inhale through the hose until the gas began to flow out. She quickly found that it was much more difficult in practice. It took multiple powerful inhales before the gas began syphoning. Once it did, Jana used the hose to spray down every inch of her living room and kitchen, taking extra care to douse all of her notebooks. She continued this, walking backwards towards her front door. She kept spraying as she walked out, creating a line of gasoline leading into her house that culminated in a pool on her front lawn.

Jana stopped to take one last look at her home, where she stored all of her anxiety, all of her paranoia, and all of her panic attacks. She put her hand in her pocket to pull out the book of matches. Slowly, as if saying goodbye one final time to an old friend, she pulled multiple matches out and struck them. And hesitantly, she dropped them into the puddle of gasoline.

She watched the flames move quickly into her home, and it wasn't long before the inside of the house was engulfed. Soon enough, she heard the neighbors walking outside, screaming and panicking. Amidst all of this, a wave of calm and closure washed over her. This was goodbye.

Chapter 13

The next day, Peter woke up with a back pain that could put down the world's strongest man. They hadn't provided him with a cot to sleep in for the duration of his stay, so he'd had to sleep on the bench inside of the cell. It was one of the most uncomfortable surfaces he'd ever had to sleep on, and that was saying something for a man that was used to sleeping on hard wood floors.

Luckily, they had been kind enough to provide him with some medical examination after his chat with Felicia. They had sent an oncologist to examine him. Given the limited medical resources of a small cell, he wasn't able to do much, but he had brought him some medications that would help ease his coughing. By the looks on the doctor's face, he knew that his cancer was getting worse, even without the use of an X-Ray or CT scan. Just as well, it wasn't like he'd be living as a free man any time soon anyway.

Peter stood up from the bench and stretched as much as he could, trying to ease the pain in his spine. He didn't know what time it was, as any time keeping device was placed facing away from him. It could be evening for all he knew. It wouldn't surprise him if he had slept for the past 24 hours, given how taxing the last few days had been for him.

Other than the oncologist, no one had come into the office to speak to him. Some people had been in and out, but no one had addressed him or asked him any questions. He was truly useless to them at this point, just like Felicia had said. That was only mildly depressing.

Peter looked down by the cell door to find that they had left a tray of food and a cup of water there for him. It was only when he laid eyes on the meal that he realized just how hungry he was. He grabbed the tray and sat down on the ground next to the bench, unwilling to put his body against that medieval torture device again until it was absolutely necessary.

The meal comprised of mashed potatoes with gravy and pieces of what he thought was turkey on top of it, a small dinner roll, some corn and the cup of water. Not exactly a feast, but it would have to do. He wasn't sure there was much more to expect from a place like this, especially for a prisoner.

Peter tried to eat it slowly and calmly, but his hunger overrode his sense of self control and he ended up devouring the meal all too quickly. His stomach was sated, but he missed the taste of food already. He didn't know how often he'd be fed, and that thought made him wish he hadn't eaten so quickly even more. What a shame.

He quickly finished the water to wash down his meal and replaced the tray and cup where it had been left for him. Maybe he'd be able to have some human contact when someone came to pick it up. More likely, they'd probably ignore any of his questions or comments and just do their job. This place was so bleak.

Peter closed his eyes and leaned back against the bench and used it to stretch and pop his back. The feeling was both satisfying and slightly painful, though it did help to ease the ache he felt there.

"Agent Craig," Peter heard someone say.

He looked forward again to see a man, somewhere in his late 20s, standing before him. He had short blond hair and was wearing a suit. He didn't look particularly physically imposing. He was short and on the skinny side. Peter thought that he was probably an analyst.

"What was that?" Peter asked, not sure if he had heard him right.

"Agent Craig. You're the one who killed him, aren't you?"

It was then that Peter noticed the look on this man's face. He looked devastated, on the verge of tears, somewhere between furious and depressed. His fists were clenched at his sides, he could tell his jaw was rigid and he was grinding his teeth.

Peter looked down in shame before he answered, "...Yeah. It was me."

"Why?" he asked.

"I..." Peter started to say that he didn't have a choice, but he knew that wasn't true. He had the choice of letting himself be arrested. He didn't have to kill a man. He chose to do it. And he couldn't lie to this man, who was clearly in pain over Peter's actions.

"Tell me why!" the man demanded, his voice now louder.

"Because... I wanted to escape. It was the only way to get away from him."

The man met his gaze, and Peter saw unmitigated fury in those eyes. This man held such rage towards Peter for what he had done.

"Craig was..." the man began, "...He was an amazing man. He didn't deserve to die. He was just doing his job, and you... you killed him in cold blood."

Peter didn't know how to respond. The man was right. Peter had done that. He hadn't known Agent Craig, but he had taken his life anyway.

"Were you related to him?" Peter asked, barely above a whisper.

"No. He was... he was my ex-husband," the man replied.

That hit Peter in the gut and almost took the breath from him. He had taken away someone that this man had obviously loved. He wasn't sure how he could live with that.

"We were going to work things out. He had called me, just before you killed him. He promised me that we were going to talk about everything. He made me a promise and you made him break it."

Peter felt tears sting the back of his eyes. He wasn't prepared for this.

"I loved him. And you took him away from me!"

Peter began to cry, feeling tears streaming down his face. He nodded in agreement with this man. He knew what he had done, and he knew there was no way to make amends for it. Peter heard the sound of a gun cocking and looked up.

This man was holding a gun up and aiming it at Peter's head. Right between his eyes. Peter simply nodded, understanding why he was about to do this.

They didn't break eye contact. Peter didn't deserve to look away. He had to see the bullet coming, and this man deserved to look the man who killed his love in the eyes as he claimed his revenge.

"I loved him..." the man said, his voice and hands both shaking.

At that moment, Felicia walked into the room and saw what was happening.

"...Rodney!" she shouted as soon as she realized what he was about to do.

She started to walk towards the man, who Peter now knew was named Rodney, in a calm fashion.

"Rodney, put the gun down," Felicia said.

Rodney's eyes didn't divert from Peter's and he made no indication of wanting to lower the gun.

"Rodney, I am ordering you to put the gun down! Now!" Felicia was shouting now.

Peter kept looking at Rodney, tears streaming down both of their faces. Peter's mouth quivered before he finally spoke, "I'm sorry."

As soon as the words left his mouth, he saw Rodney begin to pull the trigger. He heard Felicia shout something next to them but couldn't decipher what it was. The sound was drowned out by the gunshot. Before he knew it, everything went black.

***

Jeremiah sat on his couch, watching a TV show he had never heard of before. He hadn't left his house since a federal agent had dropped him off two days before. He remembered Madam Salem's words. This was the day that it would all happen.

He had spent the entire time sitting in the dark with the TV on, thinking about everything that had happened since he was in here last. He wondered if Jana would be okay when everything was said and done. He wondered about Peter. He had no way of knowing how he was doing.

Jeremiah finally stood up from his couch and made his way upstairs. He decided he needed a shower.

Jeremiah walked into his bedroom to go through his closet and pick out some clothes. He picked a simple black t-shirt, a blazer and jeans. He noticed that the towel he had used a few days before was still strewn over his bed. He hadn't been in this room since he returned home. He grabbed the towel, now dry, and walked to his bathroom.

He set the towel down near the sink and turned the water in his shower on. He set the temperature to scalding and stepped inside. He took his time to clean himself this time, savoring every moment of the water hitting his body. He had always loved his hot showers. They were so relaxing.

After twenty minutes or so, the water was starting to get cold, so he finished cleaning himself and turned it off. He opened the sliding door of his shower and reached out to grab the towel to dry himself off. As soon as he was done, he exited the bathroom, leaving the door open.

He walked into his bedroom and dropped the towel to the floor. There was no need to worry about it anymore. He rummaged through his underwear drawer to find the most comfortable briefs he had stored in there. Once he did, he pulled them on and walked to his bed where he had set out the clothes he would wear for the day.

He dressed himself and put on a pair of shoes he almost never wore. They were made to be worn with fancy three-piece suits, and he almost never had the occasion to wear them. He thought he may as well. Once he was dressed, he walked to the bathroom to brush his teeth.

He picked up his toothbrush and the tube of toothpaste next to it. He was down to the last bit of toothpaste in the tube, but it was just enough. He took his time brushing his teeth, making sure to clean them as thoroughly as he was able. Once he was done, he spit into the sink, rinsed out his mouth, looked up and took a deep breath.

He took one last look in the mirror. He looked much more tired than normal. More weathered. Like he desperately needed to sleep. With a sigh, he turned away from the mirror and walked out of the bathroom.

Jeremiah walked down the stairs and paused outside of his front door. He could see through the window that the he was still being watched by some federal agents. They had been parked outside of his home since he was dropped off. They were probably worried he would say something to the press or try to leak information. They had nothing to worry about. Jeremiah decided to just ignore them, knowing they would be following him wherever he went. He grabbed his car keys after a moment and walked outside.

He quickly made his way to his car, unlocked it, got in, put on his seatbelt and started the car. He looked out at his house through his windshield and smiled. This was the house he had bought with Sasha. The house they had shared for too brief a time. The house they were meant to grow old together in. With a sigh, he put the car into reverse and backed out of his driveway.

He knew where he was headed, and he knew it would take him a couple of hours to get there. He decided to not ruin this car ride with deliberate silence. He turned on his radio and tuned it to his favorite station. They always played his favorite music. He wasn't in the mood to sing along, but he enjoyed the accompaniment, nonetheless.

An hour and a half passed, and Jeremiah finally saw a sign indicating he was close to his destination: Monterey Bay. He took the exit that would lead him there and followed the signs carefully. It was easy to get lost in this city. The roads started and ended rather abruptly. And traffic only made it more difficult. He made sure to get into the lanes he needed to be in ahead of time.

Soon, he was driving near Monterey Bay, looking out at the ocean. The sun reflected off of the waves in an eerie and beautiful way. It was almost blinding in the way it mesmerized him. Sasha would've loved this view.

After a few more minutes of driving, Jeremiah found the parking lot for a hotel near the shore. He parked his car there, stopped it, and stepped out. He wanted to take a few more moments to take in the sights, thinking of his wife the whole time, and how much she would've loved to be here with him.

With a deep breath, he turned around and walked into the hotel behind him. The automatic doors allowed him entrance and he looked around. It was also beautiful in here. There weren't many people around. To his left, he saw a bar occupied by three people sitting alone, having a drink. They were dressed professionally, and he guessed they must be here for some sort of business meeting.

To his right was a lobby that only had one person occupying it. She was reading a book, but he couldn't make out the title of it. She was completely engrossed in it and didn't notice him looking in her direction.

After taking in the visuals, Jeremiah walked forward to the front desk.

"How can I help you?" the clerk at the desk asked.

He was a young man, early 20s, wearing the regular hotel clerk attire. He had long black hair tied into a

ponytail and his face was neatly shaven. He seemed like
a nice young man.

"I'd like a room, please. Any room will do."

"No problem. We have something on the fifth floor,
overlooking the ocean. Will that do, sir?" the young
man asked.

"Of course."

Jeremiah handed the clerk his credit card to pay for
the room and all the information necessary. After
everything was approved, he was handed the key to his
room. Jeremiah thanked the clerk and walked around
the desk to a hallway that held the elevators. He waited
for one to reach the first floor and got on it.

He was alone in the elevator. There didn't seem to be
much business for this hotel. Not a lot of people were
visiting the beach, he presumed. The elevator ride was
silent. He wondered what happened to elevator music.
He had always found it amusing.

The elevator arrived at the fifth floor, and Jeremiah
exited it quickly. He looked at signs ahead of him
telling him which direction certain numbered rooms
were. He looked down at his key and saw that he was
staying in room 519. The sign in front of him indicated
that room 519 was down the hallway on the left. He

followed the signs, and eventually came to his room. He slipped the key into the lock and opened the door.

The hotel room was neatly kept. It had a King-sized bed in the middle of two nightstands. Next to the door was a closet where he decided to store his blazer using the coat hangers they kept.

Once he was done, he made his way to the bed and sat down on it. It was one of the most comfortable beds he'd ever felt, and he wanted nothing more than to sink into it. He kicked his shoes off and pulled himself on top of the bed to lay down in a comfortable position.

Once he was laying down, he looked over at the curtains, which were shut. The clerk had said that this room overlooked the ocean. For a second, Jeremiah contemplated opening the blinds, but he decided against it. He was too comfortable and wanted to stay that way.

Before long, Jeremiah heard the sounds of crashing waves.

He heard the sounds of people panicking.

He heard explosions.

He heard inhuman shrieking that he couldn't identify.

He heard chaos happening right outside of his window. Screaming permeated his hotel room walls.

The explosions ceased, but the sounds he could only assume were coming from *them* did not. After everything, Madam Salem had been right.

There was nothing to be done.

Jeremiah closed his eyes, let out the breath he'd been holding for years, and relaxed.

The End.

Acknowledgments

First and foremost, my parents have been an anchor of support for myself and all of my endeavors throughout my life. My father, in particular, has put more emotional and financial support behind me than I probably ever deserved. He's been my biggest fan since day one, and I'll never stop appreciating him for that.

Next, are my two best friends in this world, Daniel and Savanna. For over half of our lives, they've been the ones who I could turn to for anything and with anything. The longest and most enduring non-familial relationships in my life, these two mean the world to me. It would be wrong of me not to mention them a second time.

Now I have to thank Khristine Morrow, the love of my life, who has supported me in my endeavors, as I have supported hers, since the day we met. You have given me the courage to be myself without apology.

And to all of my favorite authors, writers and novelists who inadvertently nurtured my love of literature and writing, thank you for following your dream, as I am now following mine.

Whatever is above

Whatever is below

We're caught in between

What we may never know

Made in the USA
Middletown, DE
14 September 2021

48278073R00139